—— Joe Ri......

THE ANIMAL IN AMY

Illustrated by
Roisin Bradley

First published in the UK in 2022

Belkenny Publishing

British library cataloguing is available.

ISBN 978-1-7391429-0-2

For more information visit: www.theanimalinamy.com

For my son, Adam.

To
All the children in
Peregine class at Tortworth
school,

Did you know that a
tiger's skin is as striped as
its fur? But I wouldn't
go trying to shave one!

Best wishes,

Joe R.

1
School Number Five

"You're meant to kick it."

Amy looked down at the football that had rolled to a rest against her foot, interrupting her daily lonely lap of the playground.

"Today, loser, give it here!"

"Wow, did you think of that by yourself? Aren't you a clever boy!" Amy brushed her curly red hair behind her ears and casually stepped over the ball.

"Kick it over now, **or else!**" barked the boy.

A sudden burning sensation nestled itself in the pit of Amy's stomach. She stopped, took a step back and furrowed her brow. Then, with all her might, she smashed the ball with her foot. It took off like a rocket! Whizzing through the crowd of advancing boys, it sent them scattering like pins in a bowling alley. A little smile tugged on her lips as the ball continued down the length of the playground and ripped through the net. Goal!

But it didn't stop there. The ball raced towards the school building, through a brick wall and into

the staffroom, where it bounced around like a pinball before finally stopping dead.

Every child stopped silent and gawped. Their wide eyes swung from Amy to the hole in the wall.

Suddenly, a collective gasp engulfed the playground when the principal's scowling face came into sight through the hole.

Within two whirlwind hours, Amy found herself in the backseat of her parent's car. Their bags were packed, possessions loaded into the boot and a removal van was tagging close behind. The freckles upon her cheeks would usually dance when she smiled. But as they travelled to another new town and another new school, a toothy grin was the furthest thing from her mind.

"I don't see why you couldn't just lie. Say the wind caught the ball or something."

"We've talked about this, Sweetie. People are scared of…."

"What they don't understand," drawled Amy. "I know, I know."

"Precisely, Pumpkin," replied Mum. "And why didn't you use the techniques we worked on?"

Dad stared in the rear-view mirror awaiting the response from his eleven-year-old daughter.

"There wasn't time," she replied sharply. "Plus, I didn't really want to." A tiny grin began to twitch at the corner of Amy's mouth.

"Watch the tone, young lady."

"We've got to keep your abilities a secret," smiled Mum. "And anyway, secrets can be fun."

Amy sighed theatrically as she slouched down behind the passenger seat out of view.

*

"I realise that it doesn't look like much, but I bet it's lovely inside, Coconut," insisted Mum.

'Doesn't look like much' was an understatement. School number five, Barrack Street Primary, looked like a prison. The high railings around the building were covered with so much flaking rust it was hard to tell what colour they originally were. And along the top ran razor-sharp barbed wire, undoubtedly trying to stop people from escaping rather than breaking in.

The school uniform wasn't much better. Despite Mum claiming she looked pretty, Amy most certainly did not. She looked like a melted chocolate bar in her three-tone brown outfit. It was a slight improvement from her previous school though; there the children looked like walking traffic lights.

"No way," stated Dad. "I'm not allowing my daughter to go to a place like that. Best if we return to the home-schooling."

"Dad, look, you're affecting my development," Amy argued. "Don't you want me to have a normal life? You know, with friends and hobbies and interests and learn things and..." She counted her fingers as she rhymed off her list.

"Okay, okay, enough!" he interrupted. "No need for the puppy dog eyes either. But this is it, Amy, last chance, you've no more lives left, it's all or nothing, there are no more options left." He counted on his fingers now too.

"I get it, I get it." Amy gulped as she climbed out of the car and approached her new school.

*

The Principal's office was a shrine to sport, with trophies, framed newspaper clippings and an enormous painting of himself draped in gold medals. "Good morning, Mr and Mrs Cupples, and young Amy. Please take a seat. I'm Principal Thomson. Not Thompson, no P."

"So, you don't need a pee?" smiled Amy.

"No, I don't need a pee," replied Principal Thomson sternly, narrowing his dark eyes upon the girl.

The hairs on the back of Amy's neck bristled.

She quickly pursed up her lips and sat down.

"Troublesome one we have here. Not too surprising when I look at her school record. Quite a lot of schools in such a short period of time. Never good for a child. No consistency. No discipline."
The mountain of a man took a whistle from around his thick neck and lifted it over his two croissant-like ears. He began to pace the room and swing the whistle. "Thankfully I run a tight ship. I shall personally see to it that young Amy succeeds in Barrack Street Primary. I'm sure as concerned parents, you want the same."

"Oh of course Principal Thomson," agreed Mum. "Amy is ever so bright."

"Really," interrupted the principal. "Even with all these gaps in her education."

"Ah well you see we home-schooled her," stated Dad proudly.

"And, if you don't mind me asking, what makes you qualified to do so?"

"I'm famous for my ground-breaking work in the field of zoology," said Mum.

"And I'm the world's leading herpetologist expert," added Dad.

"Animals? Insects?" chortled Principal Thomson, in his deep and gravelly voice. "What about numeracy, literacy, history? And sports?" he added, nodding towards his painting hanging proudly above his head.

"Oh, she's good at those too," stressed Mum. "Plus, she's never missed school through illness."

"Yeah, I'm never sick," agreed Amy. She couldn't recall a single occasion she had been sick. Not once, ever.

Principal Thomson wiped his wrinkled forehead that resembled a wifi symbol and shot Amy a look that again muted her instantly. "Another prime example of why this child needs to get into a class. Manners are lacking too, unfortunately. Well, she may not have been off school ill, but she's certainly been off." Principal Thomson stabbed his finger forcefully into the school report on his desk.

"We must take responsibility, Principal Thomson. Our work you see; takes us all over the country. But I'm positive we can make a go of it here at Barrack Street Primary, especially with your help."

Principal Thomson beamed proudly. "Well…."

"So, she can start on Monday?" chimed Mum, trying to press home an advantage.

"Not at all!"

Amy's heart sank.

"No time like the present," continued Principal Thomson. "A Friday in her new class will help ease her in."

2

Two Ears, One Mouth

"Be yourself. Talk up, but don't be cheeky. Let the other children get to know you. And above all stay calm, remember those new breathing exercises we worked on," whispered Mum.

"Come on Margaret, she'll be fine," said Dad, tugging on his wife's arm. "Have fun, Kiddo."

Principal Thomson led Amy's parents to the exit before marching down the corridor with the girl in tow. She passed a few smiling pupils as she chased behind his monstrous frame. A little flutter of excitement stole her breath.

Without knocking, Principal Thomson strode into a classroom. Despite the enormous shadow he threw across the room, the children were oblivious to his presence and continued talking.

"Settle down!" he grunted. "Go and find a seat, Cupples." He waved his hand to shoo her away.

Amy tentatively stepped out from behind him and stuttered in. She scanned the room for a seat. But nobody made eye contact. She lowered her head and stared at her feet.

"Sit next to me," said a boy, rushing past her into the room. She followed him to the nearest desk.

Could it be? A friend already? Amy didn't make friends easily. I mean how many children do you know that could tell you a taipan snake has enough venom to kill 100 men? Not many I presume. Granted it's a little interesting, but very depressing. And yet those were the kinds of facts Amy would often quote. Not a great conversation starter.

'I said, **settle down!"** repeated Principal Thomson, slow and purposefully.

A hush descended as he began pacing the classroom. His squeaking white trainers and piercing eyes disciplined the children.

The dark-haired boy wedged himself into his seat. He wiped away the beads of sweat gathering on his forehead. "Crisp?" he said, offering out a bag.

Amy smiled and popped one into her mouth.

"I'm Jamie."

"Amy," she whispered.

"Drink?" He pushed a bottle of coke towards her face.

Amy just shook her head and reached for another crisp.

Principal Thomson stood at the front of the room and finally addressed the class, **"Morning."**

"Good morning, Principal Thomson," they chorused in a dull monotone fashion.

"And…"

"And good morning Mrs Gallen," the class added.

Mrs Gallen stopped writing on the whiteboard and took her seat. The elderly teacher wheezed as she rested her old bones. She brushed her silver hair away from her face, scratched the wiry hairs on her chin and looked to the principal.

"Mrs Gallen, I have a new pupil, another parasite, to suck away whatever lease of life you may have remaining."

"Oh no," interrupted Mrs Gallen. "Every child is a blessing. They are wonderful."

"At making noise," insisted the principal. "You really must maintain better control over your class. Settle down!" he snapped before leaving the room.

The frail teacher began meandering between the desks towards the bookshelves, "Who would be so kind as to give out these exercise books?"

"I'll do it," offered Jamie.

"You wouldn't be offering if it were actual exercise," sniggered a blonde-haired boy at Amy's rear.

An ember began to tingle in the pit of her tummy. *Five, four, three, two, one; deep breath.*

"Thank you, Mr Hannaway," replied the teacher. "So, Amy, tell us all a little about yourself. What are your interests? Your family? Have you any hobbies?"

Amy slowly rose to her feet and cleared her throat.

Suddenly, the classroom door flew open and Principal Thomson marched back in. He surveyed the room and zoned in on Amy standing.

"Is this one causing trouble already? Didn't take you long did it?"

"No, no, no, Principal Thomson, you don't understand. Young Amy was just about to tell us something interesting."

"Oh really, in that case, do not allow me to interrupt. Do continue," replied the principal in a tone that suggested he wanted her to do anything but continue.

A cold sweat enveloped Amy. Standing in front of a new class, in a new school, was not the ideal introduction. Her mind leapt to its default setting, something she knew well and could talk about for hours.

"Did you know that rats laugh when they are tickled? And you might be interested to hear that a butterfly tastes using its feet."

Amy knew from the vacant look on the adults' faces this wasn't the interesting news they hoped for. Her classmates seemed keen though. Most nodded in agreement and some smiled.

"It may amaze you," she continued, "to discover that turtles can breathe through their bottoms."

Principal Thomson scowled and clicked his fingers. Amy instantly sat down. And the chuckles and bouncing shoulders instantly ceased.

"I'll leave you to deal with her nonsense, Mrs Gallen. Here's the reason I popped in again; a delivery for you. Please, I must insist these personal items be dealt with in your own time." He threw an enormous box of cookies onto the teacher's desk.

Mrs Gallen quickly shuffled to her desk and read aloud the note attached to the delicious-looking treats. "Thank you for all your hard work and dedication. From the grateful parents of your pupils." She glowed red as she took her seat and began to slowly nibble on a cookie.

After lunch, the classroom was loud and boisterous. Nobody was in their seat and everyone was talking. The absence of a teacher had that effect.

"Settle down! Settle down!"

yelled Principal Thomson as he strode into the room. "Take your seats and settle down!" His thick gravelly voice just made Amy wish he would cough to clear his throat.

A dainty little woman **clip-clopped** in behind the principal and made a beeline for the teacher's desk. The room was immediately filled with the sweet smell of her perfume. She placed a silver laptop on the table and peered her little green eyes over the screen to study the class. Her hair was short and dark, much like a pixie; fitting her small stature perfectly.

"Children, this is Miss Quinn. We are very fortunate that she was available to cover your class at short notice. Mrs Gallen has taken ill and won't be in for the remainder of today."

"And for the next two weeks, Principal Thomson," Miss Quinn added, with a smile.

"Two weeks?" he repeated, raising his eyebrows.

"So, I believe."

He rolled his eyes before returning his focus to the forty eyes before him, all trying endlessly to avoid his gaze. "So, it seems you have the pleasure of Miss Quinn's company for the next fortnight. I shall be calling in regularly to ensure that all is well. You see Miss Quinn, there are a few individuals in here who need to be kept in line."

"Oh, don't you worry Principal Thomson, don't let my appearance fool you. I'm no pushover." She flashed a mouthful of gleaming teeth. "I always remind children you have two ears and one mouth, so.."

"So, listen twice as much as you speak," Principal Thomson piped in.

"Exactly, and if any child fails to do so then I am certain you can assist me in dealing with their unruly behaviour."

"Oh absolutely!" He nodded in agreement. "Just bring them straight to my office."

"Well, boys and girls," started Miss Quinn, turning to address the class. "How about we start on a good note? You don't mind, do you Principal Thomson?" she whispered, lifting the left-over cookies labelled 'To Mrs Gallen.' "It would be a shame to let them go to waste."

With a smile that looked to cause him pain, the principal nodded and then sighed.

Miss Quinn weaved her way around the classroom and delicately placed a cookie on each desk. When she reached the front of the room again, she gave Amy a treat before turning to Jamie next to her. "I'm sorry young man, but there aren't any left. We did have twenty. But I assume Mrs Gallen had one."

A few children sniggered, and Jamie's eyes welled up.

"Books, desks, pupils, windows, a door," muttered Amy. "Giggling, squeaky shoes, screeching chairs, chewing." She closed her eyes, sniffed long and hard through flared nostrils, and continued, "Chocolate, Miss Quinn's perfume, sweat."

"What are you doing?" interrupted Jamie.

"It's a skill to control my emotions," she replied. "Think of five things you can see, four you can hear, three you can smell, two you can touch, then one deep breath."

"Maybe I should use that skill. Does it work?"

The tingle in her tummy had already subsided. "It does," she said, sliding her chocolate chip cookie across the table towards her friend. A twinkle in Jamie's eye made her heart leap in her chest.

That flutter abruptly fell flat when Principal
Thomson casually lifted the cookie and Jamie's drink
as he headed for the door.

"You're too kind Mr Hannaway." He threw the cookie into his pocket and went to open the bottle of coke.

"No, Sir, you can't," squeaked Jamie.

Principal Thomson's ears twitched to attention as he paused at the door.

"No?" the principal replied incredulously.

"I can't what?"

The man never took his eyes off Jamie as he began twisting the cap. Then **WHOOSH!** The liquid exploded from the bottle right into the face of Principal Thomson. Nobody dared laugh. Nobody even blinked.

"Maybe he should have let it **settle down,**" Amy whispered to Jamie. A few snorts escaped as they tried to suppress a giggle.

"You had better watch yourself, Hannaway," the principal said with a scowl. "You too Cupples." He wiped himself down and left.

"Ah Miss," called a girl at the back of the room. "Miss Quinn."

"No, no, just one cookie each I'm afraid."

"Miss Quinn," continued the girl. **"Miss!"**

"Yes, what is it?" replied the teacher who momentarily stopped fiddling with her laptop.

"Look," she pointed. "He's being sick."

"Ahh good," replied Miss Quinn. "I mean good you told me, not good he's sick. Maybe your old teacher passed on that bug. Let's go, I'm sure we can still catch Principal Thomson."

The small-framed teacher hurried towards the boy vomiting in the sink and quickly ushered him out of the room.

When she did eventually return, her visit was fleeting. A very apologetic girl called Farrah discovered that 'checking the time' was not to be a valid excuse for using a mobile in class. Within moments, Miss Quinn had spun on her heels, confiscated the phone, and began marching the trembling girl towards the principal's office.

Very little teaching took place for the remainder of the day. What little time Miss Quinn did spend in the classroom was evenly distributed between dishing out textbooks and tapping keys on her laptop.

Amy and Jamie certainly didn't complain. They spent most of the day chatting. And by three o'clock Amy floated out of school, beaming so much her very cheeks were sore. *A cruel principal and a tummy bug were small sacrifices for a new friend. Roll on Monday!*

3
Simon Visits

"Well then, come on, how was it?"

"Fine," smiled Amy as she climbed into the car. "What's this?" she asked pulling something out from below her.

"It's your new booster seat," smiled Dad.

"Not funny," she replied sternly. "It weighs a ton."

"It's just an old work laptop. No use in the office so I'm taking it home," said Mum.

Amy slid the huge black box to the other side of the car; she admired the animal stickers on the laptop and put her seatbelt on.

"Fine? That's all I'm getting?" shrugged Mum. "So, what did you get up to?"

"Nothing really. It was fine," replied Amy, choosing her words carefully. The last thing she wanted was to give her Dad an excuse to stop her from returning.

"Six hours a day in one building and you did nothing?"

Amy needed to give them something. Dad still hadn't started the car as he awaited details.

"Ohhh, who's that?" questioned Mum, spying a boy frantically waving at the car.

"It's Jamie."

"Ohhh, Jamie, a friend? Well that's something, isn't it," grinned Mum.

"And the teacher?" asked Dad. "Mrs Gallen."

"It's not her anymore?"

"It's not?" replied Dad, a seriousness to his tone.

"It's Miss Quinn now. Mrs Gallen went home sick. Another boy in the class caught it too. A tummy bug I think."

"Well, aren't we fortunate your abilities stop you from getting ill." Dad winked at his daughter in the mirror as he started up the engine.

"Right, now what shall we have for our Friday takeaway?"

BRRIINNNGGG BRRIINNGGG

Mum picked up her mobile phone. Amy watched on with intrigue as Mum's eyes grew as wide as the smile on her face. She began patting Dad's shoulder causing him to sway on the road.

"Yes, yes, of course. We'd be delighted. Tonight? No problem at all. Thank you, no thank you. Goodbye, bye-bye."

"What is it, Margaret? Who was it?"

"That was only the head of the Borneo research facility. She wants us to fly out, tonight, for two weeks of intensive work with their endangered orangutans."

"I'm not going," sulked Amy, cutting into the conversation.

"You have no choice, Sweetie," said Dad. "Anyway, this is the opportunity of a lifetime."

"But Dad, what about school, and Jamie?"

"It's only two weeks, Peanut, it'll fly by."

"Well, I'm not going!"

"No arguing," replied Dad. "It's a trip to Borneo or two weeks with your cousins. And we know how that went last time."

Before focusing on saving endangered animals Amy's parents were proper scientists, with white coats and microscopes. Amy didn't know much about their work, but the storeroom at their office was always full of old equipment, including an old enormous fridge freezer. Her cousins, Clare and Cleo, thought it funny to trap Amy inside- with the appliance turned on!

"Remember how angry that made you?" Dad added.

"Yeah but I was fine," replied Amy.

"The North American Tree Frog," Mum whispered to Dad.

"What's that?" asked Amy, sticking her head between the front two seats of the car.

"Nothing, Popcorn. Well, I suppose it is only two weeks," said Mum, turning to Dad. "And she has just started school. It would be a shame to leave it already. Especially when she has settled in."

"Okay, okay," sighed Dad. "But I want you to be sensible, young lady."

"Me? No problem. I'm always sensible," she said brightly.

"Yeah as sensible as a cup holder on a roller-coaster," replied Dad.

*

As much as Amy detested her cousins, leaving school and ruining a friendship before it even began was worse. Clare and Cleo were identical twins, inside and out. They were thirteen years old and extremely tall for their age. They had shocking blonde hair, and green eyes and neither was ever without a mobile phone in their hands. Perhaps it was their age or their size, but they almost thought it was their duty to pick on Amy. Their dad, Uncle Jack, wasn't much better. He saw no bad in his little girls. Clearly love is blind for they certainly weren't little, and they most definitely were bad.

Sitting around a dining room table with enough food to feed a small army, Amy reached for the bowl of French fries.

"Hey! Hands off twerp!" said Cleo as she stabbed Amy's outstretched hand with a fork drawing blood.

"Ooweeee! That hurt!"

"Serves you right, loser," said Clare. "Stick to the vegetables. We don't want those."

Daring not to cry in front of her vile cousins, Amy tucked her quivering bottom lip into her mouth.

"Best you go clean that up in the bathroom," advised Uncle Jack. "There's only one red liquid I want on my chips and it isn't your blood."

She raced to the bathroom and forced her hand under hot gushing water. It stung worse than the initial stabbing. A sudden fury flooded Amy's body like she'd jumped into a hot tub. She grasped the sink with both hands and stared at her teary eyes in the mirror. A warm itch was now racing through her body towards her cut hand.

Turning the water off she noticed something peculiar. She stared at her wound. The blood had stopped oozing and new skin was already growing over the puncture before her very eyes. "I just regenerated again. Like a scarlet jellyfish." She held her breath and covered her mouth. A little twinkle lit up her eyes and a sly grin danced upon her thin lips.

Suddenly three enormous burps reverberated around the house. *How can I possibly put up with that lot for two whole weeks?* But *I must, for Jamie!* The anger swelled again in her tummy. She longed to be invisible, unseen, and untouched for a fortnight. She reached for a towel to clean her bloody hand before wiping her face clear of any tears.

"Hurry up in there! You have to do the dishes!" her Uncle hollered from the kitchen.

The burning fury ferociously shot around her body. Amy drew a deep breath and took a final look in the mirror. *You can do this!* Only she wasn't in the mirror. There was no reflection. She was completely and utterly see-through, except for the school uniform that she was still in. Invisible goose pimples raced up her arms. Or at least that is what she hoped they were.

Can you imagine having the superpower of invisibility? Just being able to disappear at will, sneak into the cinema to watch some free movies, stay locked up in a toy shop overnight, and imagine the pranks you could play! In an instant, Amy compared her new power to that of a ghost shrimp. This little freshwater creature is almost completely transparent, only visible really after eating some colourful food. She knew exactly what to do with this new 'talent'.

So, began the haunting of the Howards.

She returned from the bathroom, but the Howards didn't know that. Now invisible she began making food dance in the air before launching it towards the ceiling. She poured a jug of water over her uncle, stuck Clare's hand into the mayonnaise, and put Cleo's long blonde ponytail into the ketchup.

Next, she played with everything in the kitchen. Water taps on and off; the microwave went ding, the oven door opened then shut and all the cupboards slammed without explanation.

When Amy, now visible, returned from the bathroom, the family was in the middle of an argument. The finger of blame was passed around the table, until, Amy casually remarked,

"You lot look like you have seen a.."

"A ghost!" interrupted Uncle Jack. "It was a ghost, moving things, opening cupboards, making noise. It was a ghost I tell you."

"A poltergeist ghost to be exact," Amy said, calmly. "I've seen this before." She sat back and enjoyed as a cloud of fear reigned over the family dinner.

Lying in bed that night it occurred to Amy that yet again emotions had triggered an ability. *Do my parents know about this one? Do they have the same abilities?* she pondered. Mum and Dad had always been honest. They continuously told her that her abilities had been developing since she was a baby. But that little nugget of information was always followed with a reminder to hide what you can do.

If only she could control the boiling blood that bubbled in her stomach, then she could repeat the feat and vanish again. Just one more prank and the Howard family would be rushing around after her faster than a hummingbird flaps its wings- which is approximately 80 times per second by the way.

It didn't take much to fuel the anger again. The difficulty was choosing a specific incident to recall. Staring at the stab wound on her hand a tingle passed through Amy's body and her very eyes began to quiver. She took a long deep breath and focused on catapulting the fiery fury down to her fingertips and every single toe. She cautiously opened her eyes and dared to wave her hand in front of her face. A hand she could no longer see. Silently she crept over to the mirror to confirm what she already knew. She was indeed invisible, again. And she'd controlled it.

While the family was fast asleep in bed, Amy crept out and began. She started with Cleo's bedroom. Both twins were sharing a bed, tops to tails. Another reason they disliked Amy so much- she'd been given Clare's room to stay in. She started small; just subtly opening and closing drawers and wardrobes. Amy was clever about how she'd play the prank. Slow and steady. Like a dripping tap, it would eventually wear you down until snap!

Clare was the first to wake up. She shuffled up the bed to get next to her sister. Then the flashing lights began. Amy was finding it hard work running around the room. But by the growing look of horror on Clare's face, it was becoming worth it.

"Get up! Get up! Get up!"

she screamed, pulling at her dozing twin.

"What is it?" Cleo replied groggily.

"It's back! Look! The ghost's back!"

Amy started to fling books across the room, open and shut the window, and made Cleo's wrestling figures float in mid-air. The invisible girl was having so much fun that she was now cackling like never before. That only added to the terrifying scene for the twin sisters, who by now, were clinging together so tightly they looked like two squished marshmallows.

The moment Amy put on a nightdress belonging to her larger cousin and began dancing around the room, the two sisters launched themselves towards the door and into their Dad's room.

Amy gave chase. The two trembling sisters leapt upon their father. Uncle Jack yelped like a little girl the second he saw a nightdress floating around his room. Amy circled the bed all the while fighting hard not to giggle and give herself away. She then slowly, and purposefully, began knocking ornaments off the shelves one by one. Each time a little figure smashed into the wooden floor her uncle squealed. It gave Amy so much pleasure to see these horrible bullies so fearful.

Uncle Jack gritted his teeth, grabbed his girls, and made a bolt for the stairs.

Amy swiftly returned to her room and pretended to be awoken by the sweet screams of panic. Uncle Jack, as white as...well a ghost, was slicing the air with a mop and the twins were clinging on to one another for dear life. Amy sauntered into the kitchen beaming with pride.

"What are you grinning about, child?!" barked her Uncle. "It's obvious it's that ghost again."

"I know," she replied, coolly. "It's Simon. I did say I had seen this before. He always turns up when people are nasty to me."

"He does? Really? Did you hear that girls?" shrieked her uncle. "When people are nasty to her. So, I will have no more. Nothing but kindness from now on, only the best for your cousin, Amy. In fact, stop gawping and go make her breakfast."

4
PE Lesson

"Tardiness will not be tolerated," bellowed Miss Quinn as Darren strolled into the room. "Let's go and see what Principal Thomson has to say about this."

When she returned some twenty minutes later, Miss Quinn was grinning from ear to ear.

"It is a lovely gesture, ever so thoughtful."

"The parents are soft if you ask me," replied Principal Thomson, following her into the room.

"Look boys and girls," she began, "more cookies. You really must thank your parents when you get home. In fact, let me share the kindness." She began distributing the treats around the classroom.

A din quickly began to spread across the room, much to the annoyance of the towering principal.

"That's enough! Settle down, it's time for PE everyone."

As Amy and her class trudged slowly outside it took all her willpower not to tell Jamie about the prank she played on the Howards over the weekend. *Could she trust him with such a secret so soon in their friendship? Would he think she was a freak?*

There stood seventeen unfortunate souls in a lumpy and shapeless field, surrounded by nettles and trees. The 'pitch' was used by the school for all PE lessons, sports days, and even playground time when it was dry.

Miss Quinn, a notebook in hand, prowled the sorry-looking line of children tutting throughout. Many looked an unhealthy shade of green, Mrs. Gallen's tummy bug seemed to be still circulating.

Although the rain had eased off, it was still drizzling, and this, along with the pitiful PE kits the children wore, made the scene more wretched. Amy felt the water dripping down her naked arms but unlike the rest, she didn't have any goose-bumps. She considered her remarkable tolerance for the cold to be like a North American flat bark beetle. That little insect's body contains antifreeze proteins allowing it to live in temperatures as low as minus fifty-eight degrees Celsius. *Was it another ability?* Certainly not a superpower that anyone would be requesting but a power, nonetheless. Perhaps triggered by the anger slowly inching over her body caused by the blonde-haired bully, Conor Phillips, who at every opportunity threw her a deathly stare.

Amy was never particularly fond of PE lessons. She wasn't especially quick and never managed to catch anything thrown at her. But of late, with the powers, maybe things were to change. However, the dread of PE and its reality hit her square in the face when she saw Principal Thomson strut towards the class with a sack of equipment tossed over one shoulder. The rain never saturated his body but instead bounced off his muscles.

"Before you begin Principal Thomson, Maya here has a sore leg and can't participate."

"And I bet she hasn't a note," he snorted. "Would you please escort her to my office? I shall deal with her later." He narrowed his beady eyes and clenched a fist before returning his attention to the class.

Miss Quinn replied with an awkward wince and scurried off.

"Right, half of you over there, take that side," Principal Thomson barked, tossing a long thick rope. "And you lot on the other side," he added, pointing at the remaining eight children nearest him. "Tug of war. The first team to pull their opponents past me wins."

Amy and Jamie quickly scampered to the same side and moved into position. Amy, her face closed with worry, stood behind Jamie. It was obvious he disliked PE more than her. She gave him a reassuring pat on the back.

"Ah come on, Sir. These teams are unfair," moaned Conor. "They've got all the weight on their side."

Amy felt a fury creep down her arms and tickle the palms of her hands. Her eyebrows lowered, and she gritted her teeth. White knuckled, she grasped the rope and readied herself.

Principal Thomson ignored the remarks from the class bully and continued, **"Ready, take the strain, annnnddd PULL!"**

The sixteen children pulled and tugged with all their might. But there was only ever going to be one outcome, and it wasn't due to a weight difference. Amy snatched the rope. Yanked it towards her. Then let loose. The rope shot through the air, flailing like a windmill; with Conor and his teammates still attached. The defeated team slowly clambered to their feet, unsure of how exactly they ended up twenty metres away.

Jamie, blowing on his rope-burnt hands, spun around to Amy. Wide-eyed, a broad smile lit up his face.

Amy's heart was pounding so hard against her chest it was hurting. *Had she just revealed an ability to everyone? Would they know it was her?*

"Was that you," whispered Jamie.

"Dung beetle," she stuttered.

"A what?"

"A dung beetle," she replied. "They can move weights one thousand times their body weight."

Miss Quinn raced back to the field; her eyes large with intrigue. Frantically taking notes she moved closer to the principal as he led the group towards the start line for a race. While his methods were unorthodox, and barbaric even, Principal Thomson certainly managed to motivate the children. What followed next was a set of events contested so ferociously you would be mistaken for thinking there was an Olympic medal up for grabs.

The sprint heats were run at a school record time. Principal Thomson was even ruffling the hair of those who impressed him. Shocked, the children slowly moved away beyond his reach, fixed their hair, and scratched their heads. By the time her turn came around Amy was twitching with restlessness. She stood on the start line, with Jamie to her left and Conor Phillips on her right. The whistle blew.

Amy dashed off the chalked line. With her red ponytail flapping in the wind she gracefully raced ahead. Suddenly her ankles were clipped, and both feet clattered into each other. Lying on the ground she looked up quickly enough to hear Conor laugh as he barged into Jamie and sent him tumbling to the dirt. Fire shot through Amy. She exploded to her feet and moved so fast that her feet barely touched the ground. She won, comfortably, leaving her opponents, and Conor, in a literal cloud of her dust. Miss Quinn, still taking notes, yelled out her time. Amy's heart leapt into her mouth. What would they do? How would they react?

"That's it, everyone, inside!" Principal Thomson yelled. "Well done, everyone!"

Well done? A compliment. The children moved cautiously towards the large man. *Was it a trap? Was he really in a good mood?* The stupefied class forced an uneasy smile as they passed the principal who was now holding the door open and patting heads.

"Watch your back!" grunted Conor as he rushed past throwing a shoulder into Amy. Jamie caught her as she stumbled.

"Hurry, hurry, lots to do." Principal Thomson was now clapping and smiling.

Amy approached the door, "Thank you."

"Oh no, thank you, child," he said. "This is the one, Miss Quinn; this child can win every athletic event for Barrack Street Primary."

"Well done child," added Miss Quinn.

Amy shuddered as all the unwanted attention was lavished upon her.

"Yes, well done, Amy." Principal Thomson spat out the compliment as if it were painful. He slapped her on the back. "Wait a second!" he added, pulling Amy back by the collar of her t-shirt.

Amy recoiled, her skin crawling.

"What are those on your neck?" he asked.

"The scars?" replied Amy. "Always had them. Don't know how."

"Spider or snake?" the teacher interjected.

"Eh?"

"Miss!" came a yell from inside the school. "Miss, Paul's just been sick."

Amy was grateful for the distraction, Miss Quinn and Principal Thomson darted inside and broke the hungry stare they had fixed upon her.

Once inside Amy found herself being hauled by Jamie into the nearest toilets.

"These are the boys!" she sniffed.

"It's fine," he replied as he checked each cubicle. "They're empty. So come on, tell me, how's it work?"

"How's what work?" she replied, looking to the ground.

Jamie was jittery with excitement, hopping from one foot to the other. "What else can you do? Are you like a super girl trying to live an ordinary life? Is that why you've come to our school? It doesn't get any more ordinary than here."

Amy traced her tongue around her lips. "I think you've read too many comics." She giggled nervously.

"It's okay you can trust me," Jamie said solemnly. "I mean who am I going to tell anyway? You're my only friend in this dump."

"Well," she began. "I can do a few things. Superhuman things I suppose," she confided. "Happens when I get emotional. It's just a shame I won't be around to show you."

"Why not?" asked Jamie, in a high-pitched tone. "What do you mean? Are you leaving?"

"I don't plan to. But once my parents return from work and get wind of me using my powers, they'll pull me out of school, again." She bit her bottom lip. "Wait a second, I know what we can do."

"Go on," smiled Jamie, leaning in.

"They are away for two weeks, that gives us time to fix things, and maybe I'll get to stay."

"Fix things?"

"Don't you think it's a bit suspicious?" Amy began. "All the children going to Principal Thomson's office and none of them has come back. He's up to something. I mean I've never seen a principal in the classroom so much in my life."

"Yeah, now you mention it. He's never usually like that. What do you think he's doing?"

"I wish I knew."

"Well then there's only one thing we can do?" said Jamie.

"Use these powers and find out what he's at?" Amy replied brightly.

"Well I was going to say get a snack, but yes that's a good idea too," smiled Jamie. "So, am I the only one who knows about them?" he asked hopefully.

"Just you and my parents. And I think they know a bit more than they are letting on."

"What makes you think that?"

"Just the other day they mentioned the North American Tree Frog."

"The what?"

"It's a frog that can freeze itself all winter then thaw out in the springtime when there's lots of food."

"Not sure I want that power. Although, waking up when there's lots of food does sound nice," he laughed.

"So, you fancy helping me learn how to control these powers? Then we can sort Principal Thomson. Maybe even keep him quiet so my parents will be none the wiser about anything."

"I think we need to," replied Jamie, "otherwise we could be next."

5
Haircut

"I do wish you would stop scratching your head, Christopher," said Miss Quinn, throwing an intrigued eye over her laptop. "It really isn't nice."

"I can't help it, Miss," he responded, digging all ten fingers into his scalp. "Can I go to the toilet?"

"I'm afraid not, that could be lice and we don't want them to spread."

The three children around Christopher instantly pushed their chairs away. **"Ewww!"**

The teacher picked up her handbag and headed for the door, "Come on, I'll let Principal Thomson make the call on this one. Workbooks out! Not a word until I return."

Amy furrowed her brow as she observed Miss Quinn march another pupil down the corridor towards the principal's office. "It's him again!" she whispered to Jamie. "Look! He's got rid of another one."

"Come on, how?" Jamie replied incredulously as he withdrew crisps from his schoolbag.

"Remember he was ruffling everyone's hair at PE? He's planted something. I just know it."

"Well, we're fine, and that PE was great. So, success all round if you ask me."

"That PE was great?" she replied in a high-pitched voice.

"Yeah! The best in weeks. I was on a team that won, and I didn't have to run once," he laughed.

"That's because you were pushed over."

"Like I said, never ran once," Jamie grinned.

Amy shared the giggle before stopping to scan the room and study the many empty desks around her. "Surely, they can't all need to be sent home," she mused.

Sitting at the front of the room, Amy was suddenly fully aware of the uneasy silence behind her. Jamie stopped crunching his crisps and they held one another's gaze. To their rear, a plan was afoot. The question was who would be the victim?

SWISH! A pair of metal scissors whistled through the air. Then Amy's ponytail was suddenly yanked and SNIP!

"I told you to watch your back," bellowed Conor Phillips, proudly brandishing a pair of scissors, their sharpness reflecting the classroom lights. "But hey, at least I've saved you a haircut." He began howling with laughter.

The rest of the class sat in shocked silence. A few forced out a stuttering laugh only when the blonde-haired bully, Conor, caught their eye.

Amy's luscious red hair fell to the ground in parallel with her tears. Distraught, she stumbled out of her seat and bent down to gather the remains of hair from the ground. Heavy-legged she fell back into her chair, feeling the strange sensation of the cold classroom air whip around her head.

Jamie rubbed her shoulder as she sat down, "It's okay, don't be sad. I know, tell me five things you can see…"

"It's…it's…too late," she blubbered.

A heaviness smothered her body like a cosy blanket. Her bottom lip quivered uncontrollably, and she was teetering on the edge of a full-body shaking sob.

The classroom door suddenly flew open. **"What's going on in here?"** yelled Miss Quinn, breathless and sweaty. "Why are you crying child?" She moved closer to Amy's table and noticed the pile of hair clippings. "Who did this?" she asked, holding up the hair.

Nobody replied. Not even Jamie. He knew better and didn't want to be next.

Amy tucked in her bottom lip and took a long deep breath. The fizz in her tummy had not subsided. Instead, it raced to her head. She let out a little yelp as she felt a sharp pain like someone had tugged her hair, again. She swung her head around to stare at Conor.

Miss Quinn paced the room with a handful of hair. The palpable silence in the class was quickly replaced with frantic whispers and pointing.

"What did you do, child? Is this a prank?"

Amy glanced around through glassy eyes and found everyone ogling her. She nervously reached for her hair and began twisting it around her fingers. And it was there. Amazingly, all her long red hair was there! Every curl was thicker and longer than before.

Amy wiped away her tears and replaced them with an enormous grin. *Another ability! Another superpower!*

Miss Quinn shook herself back into life, "I don't believe it. I have only ever seen this before in a white-tailed deer."

"You mean the type that can re-grow antlers?" Amy asked.

Amy was twitching with information. When she wasn't reading a book or watching a nature program on television, she'd drift off into her own little documentary, narrating the activities of any creatures in sight.

"Exactly, child. Or perhaps a gecko or starfish who can regrow limbs."

"Salamanders can regenerate too," Amy added.

"Bright child," complimented the teacher. "You know your animals."

The compliment felt like a well-needed hug around her. And Jamie's encouraging smile made her eyes well up.

"I assume all this knowledge is down to your parents — scientists, aren't they? Margaret and Patrick?"

"Yeah, how did you know?"

"It's all here, in this data collection sheet," she replied waving a sheet of paper. Miss Quinn began carefully placing Amy's cut-off hair into a poly pocket that she stapled closed.

"Can I have that?" asked Amy gesturing toward her sealed hair.

"It's of no use now. Best I dispose of it," replied the teacher, smiling.

BRRINNNGGGG

"Okay, out you go. I'll see you all tomorrow."

"Good afternoon, Miss Quinn," chimed the wide-eyed children as they exited, all the while pointing at Amy's long new ponytail.

6
Control the Powers

"Have you had a snack yet? Can I get you a sandwich?"

"No, I'm okay," replied Amy.

"What kind of sandwich would you like?"

"Really Jamie, I'm fine."

"Want a chicken sandwich?"

"Honestly it's okay. I'm not that hungry."

"Yeah, I'll get us a chicken sandwich. It's no bother."

Amy smiled as Jamie headed for the bedroom door. Looking around her she was beginning to feel that meeting Jamie had been fate. His room was plastered in Superhero paraphernalia- posters, clocks, comics, figures, bedsheets. There was no one better to help her to perfect her abilities.

He returned with two plates and a mountain of sandwiches. "Not sure if you wanted mayonnaise. So, this plate is plain," he said holding aloft a plate. "And this plate has mayo."

"I love your room," gushed Amy. "I never live anywhere long enough to decorate a room."

"Yeah, why do you keep moving school?"

"It's my parents' work. We are always moving, all over the country. They say it's because of their work, they always claim they have to go to where they are needed, where animals need help. But it's mainly to hide my abilities. Once I've revealed a power, we are on the road again; moving quickly to avoid attention and questions."

"Superpowers you mean," interrupted Jamie.

"Yeah superpowers," she beamed.

"You know; people can fear the unusual."

"Is that from one of your comics?" Amy asked, tracing a finger over the pile on the shelf.

"Not really. But, with great power comes great responsibility."

"That's definitely from a comic."

"It is, Spiderman," laughed Jamie. "But it's true. Maybe your parents didn't want people experimenting on you or something."

"You're reading too many of these." She tossed a comic onto the bed. "Right, let's practice using these so-called superpowers then."

Jamie didn't even bother to finish his sandwich and trailed Amy out of the room.

*

The duo stood in the neglected back garden. The grass was overgrown, and a rusty swing nestled itself at the bottom next to a broken bench. A few discarded footballs peeked over the grass in hope that they may be kicked.

Jamie stood with a clipboard, pen, and stopwatch. He slowly paced the length of the garden, counting aloud, and then made a few calculations.

"Okay, we obviously need to keep this a secret. So, we can't very well go to the park and test your powers, this will have to do." He began circling Amy like he was her superior in the army. "I see my brother still hasn't cut the grass. That will be taken into consideration when I calculate your speed."

"You know how to do that?"

"I do, easy numeracy."

Amy went red and looked to the ground.

"I mean it's not that easy" assured Jamie. "I'm just really good at maths. I can show you anytime."

Amy's face lit up as she backed up towards the house. Unsure exactly why but she squatted in the runner's position and took a deep breath.

"Ready?" shouted Jamie, standing by the fence at the bottom of the garden, stopwatch in hand.

"Ready!" replied Amy.

"Go!" he blasted.

"No wait," said Amy, standing up. She walked toward her friend. "It won't work."

"Why not?" he asked, puzzled. "You did it in PE."

"Yeah, but I was angry then."

"And in class?" he quizzed.

"Well, then I was upset. Remember, being emotional triggers my abilities. But I've got good at controlling my emotions, and so my abilities too."

"Good?" smirked Jamie.

"Okay maybe not good, but I have got better. Another technique is to name the emotion and then do the opposite reaction."

"Well don't do that now," screeched Jamie. **"I need you annoyed, go on, get upset, get angry...you....you lazy....smelly girl."**

Amy started laughing, then paused to sniff her shirt. Jamie tried to keep a stern face, but his snort released a belly-bouncing giggle.

"Ahh has the little boy not got any friends?" he began. "Poor Jamie. You loner!"

"Ehey?" asked Amy, wearing a quizzical look.

"Sorry, that's what they say to me. I meant to change the words." He solemnly looked to his feet.

Amy felt a sudden twinge in her tummy bubble and spew over. She darted back to the house, resumed her position, and yelled, "I'm ready!"

"Go!"

She raced down the garden with such velocity that the swing nearly completed a full loop as she sped past. The grass shot back and forth as she burned a trail through and ventured towards her friend. She saw him glance at the watch then his smiling eyes caught Amy's. But she had failed to remember one very important fact. Something that could be very damaging. Braking distance! She hadn't given herself any. She forcefully dug her heels into the ground. The smell of the burning rubber soles didn't fill her with any confidence. The wooden fence was nearing. Five metres, four metres, Jamie leapt aside, into the nettles and out of sight, three metres, two, one,

WALLOP!

Amy punctured the fence, raced through the neighbour's washing line, and finally came to a stop squished against the neighbour's shed with a pair of old lady's underpants covering her like a Halloween mask.

She staggered back towards Jamie and through the little girl shape hole she'd left in the fence.

"I don't think that's quite the right superhero costume for you," smirked Jamie.

Amy chuckled as she threw the cream underpants back towards the washing line. "So?" she asked. "What was the speed?"

Jamie picked the final few thorns from his neck and began writing on his clipboard. "Ahem, it looks like it was, roughly, almost, but not exactly.."

"Yes, yes, come on?" she pressed, dancing on the spot.

"At best guess, I would say, nearly 65 miles per hour!"

"65 miles per hour," she gasped. "You know what that is? That's only the speed of one of the world's fastest animals- a cheetah."

"A cheetah? You can run as fast as a cheetah?" he gurgled, still finding thorns in his scalp. "So, you must have found a trigger. What was it? Was it thinking of evil Principal Thomson or are you sad because you miss your parents?"

Amy's eyes twinkled. "Yeah, something like that," she replied coolly.

"Jamie!" came a holler. "Dinner's ready."

7
Seamus

Sure, Amy could have raced home and got there in minutes, but why subject herself to a more torturous time with her cousins? Instead, she dawdled, collecting her thoughts, and considering her next move. To keep Jamie a friend and avoid a permanent return to home-schooling she needed to get to the bottom of what Principal Thomson was doing with all the children. And of course, she needed to stay calm and avoid using any more abilities in school.

The streets were quiet and empty, save for the odd car that rumbled by as it tackled each of the carefully placed speed bumps. The car's engine was matched only by the sound her tummy was making. She regretted not eating Jamie's sandwich. **RUMBLE!**

She crossed the road and neared the last few streets before she'd be home. Weighed down by her school bag she almost toppled over as she tied a loose lace. Whilst crouching she heard the most horrible of sounds. Amy clenched her stomach to silence it and pricked her ears. A dog! That sound though. Not a bark for food, or a howl for attention. This was an ear-piercing cry for help; distinct and undeniable.

Amy darted over to a lonely custard yellow-coloured house at the end of a terraced row and peered in the window. Nothing. She followed the sound to the rear of the house and peeked into the kitchen. Her breath shortened, and her heart pounded in her chest with such force she thought it may burst out. A panicked terror coiled itself around her body and shot through her veins.

She found the most humungous Irish wolf hound choking to death on his collar. The frighteningly large dog was so tall that he had managed to get his collar hooked on the handle of the back door. His struggle had succeeded only in wedging the piece of leather tighter and tighter around his neck.

She needed in, and fast. But she couldn't use her strength to kick the door in. That may kill the dog. And she couldn't force open the front door because a neighbour might see her use her powers. She frantically scoured the rear of the building. An open window! With only one snag, it was upstairs.

Amy bolted to the drainpipe and began to shimmy up the web-covered plastic pipe. She hadn't much experience. The absence of friends meant she had spent little time climbing trees, walls, or railings. She had just passed the lower windows and was gaining confidence with each inch she scaled. *I bet this would impress Jamie,* she thought. The yelps of the dog spurred her on. The open window was just a fingertip away.

CREAK!

The drainpipe moaned under Amy's weight. She dared not move.

SNAP!

The bolts securing the pipe to the wall began popping out one by one. **POP, POP, POP!** Like the buttons of an ill-fitting shirt.

"Arrgghhhh," she screamed, hurdling towards the ground.

CRASH!

Amy hit the ground, back first, but felt no pain. The stirring emotions over-rode any pain and the squeals of the dog were drowning out any other sound. A mixture of worry, panic, and anger saw her spring up. She scurried back to the window. The dog was beginning to wobble on his feet.

Amy drew back a few paces, ran towards the house, and threw herself into the air towards the window. She made it! Teetering precariously on the window ledge she froze. *Now that would impress Jamie. A grasshopper maybe? They can jump twenty times their body length.* But she didn't have time to surmise the origin of her new ability.

She frantically climbed inside and ran down the stairs, through the sitting room and towards the kitchen. It was locked. Who locks a kitchen door? Abilities didn't have to be summoned; her tinted cheeks revealed her emotions for all to see. With her strength, she prized the door open. Inside Amy swiftly unhooked the dog's collar from the door handle and watched as he collapsed to the ground panting.

She fell to her knees and threw her arms around the dog to comfort him. Still gasping and with his tongue hanging out she ran to get him a drink. She bit her bottom lip when she found his bowl empty of water. *Some people don't deserve dogs*. She lifted his heavy head and placed the water bowl under his chin. His dog tag clinked as he slurped like he'd never had a drink before. Amy read the tag as the mountain of a dog finally climbed to his feet. 'Seamus.' He rested his head on Amy's shoulder.

"You're welcome," she whispered, as she scratched his neck.

Suddenly Seamus withdrew his head and backed off into the corner of the room, quivering. Amy heard keys in the front door. Still fuming she opened the kitchen door and began to march towards the dog's owner, prepared to give whomever it was a piece of her mind! But as she strode through the sitting room she paused.

GULP.

She scanned the room- the pictures, the trophies, even a treadmill perched in the corner. She knew the owner only too well and silently backed away. She retreated into the kitchen with Seamus, catching a passing glimpse of herself in a full-length mirror, all the colour had drained from her face.

8
Bird Cloud

Principal Thomson, lumbered down with countless bags of shopping, staggered into the kitchen, and settled his groceries on the worktop. After a quick rummage around in a bag, he withdrew a packet of cooked ham.

"Want some, boy?" he gestured towards the dog. Seamus perked up and stood to attention. "Well tough!" he rasped. The cruel principal rolled the entire pack of ten slices up and scoffed them down in one. The shaggy grey dog shrank back into his corner, crestfallen.

Wedged into a small utility room behind a tumble dryer and concealed behind a collection of brushes and mops, Amy kept a watchful silence through a crack in the open door as Principal Thomson busied himself dumping all the shopping out of their bags and onto the worktop.

Amy's eyes widened. "Cookies!" she mouthed. *I knew it!* Packs and packs of them.

The principal was out of control, like a kite in a hurricane. He began launching food items away with such aggression that each slamming drawer, cupboard, and fridge made Amy jolt.

This was the time she needed to be invisible; to use an ability. Forget pranking family; this is where it would count. This was life or death. But she couldn't.

She was fully dressed. He'd spot the horrid brown uniform in an instant.

"Breathing board," the trembling girl whispered to herself.

She began to trace a square on the palm of her left hand using her right index finger. She'd breathe in as she drew one side of the square and exhaled on the next side. Over and over she went, square after square, breath after breath. It worked. She felt calmer, in control, ready to stay hidden and wait it out. Despite the situation, she found herself in, Amy's chest puffed out a little when she thought how proud Mum would be.

All of a sudden, the utility room door flung open. Squishing Seamus in the process. The neglected dog yelped but was silenced with a raise of Principal Thomson's fist. The principal strode into the room and tossed a multipack of toilet rolls on top of the tumble dryer. The rolls slid off the dryer, hit the brushes, and sent three to the ground. Principal Thomson grunted in annoyance. The veins were throbbing under the skin in his muscly arms.

Amy, now cowering behind the remaining brushes, quivered as he neared her. If he looked in her direction, if he even sniffed in her direction, she was done for.

The enormous man picked up the brushes and tossed them carelessly back into the corner of the room. Then kicked the toilet rolls to the rear of the cupboard before rumbling out and slamming the door behind him.

Amy finally exhaled, and her tense body relaxed. *That was the last brush with death I want*, she thought as she climbed out from her hiding spot.

The moment she heard her principal thunder upstairs she made good her escape out the back door. But not before opening the fridge and tossing Seamus a whole, already cooked, roast chicken.

With her nerves beginning to settle and her heart rate returning to normal, she headed for the nearest route out through some trees. Her mind was racing with thoughts, questions and theories. But when she saw hundreds of birds take to the sky as she waded through their home, one protruding idea sprung to mind- a way to teach Principal Thomson a lesson.

She didn't sleep much that night. Instead, she lay like a starfish on her bed with a satisfying smile on her face because she saved Seamus the dog. But now she needed to do something about Principal Thomson.

The moment the morning sun broke into her room, Amy stealthily crept downstairs, filled a plastic bag with bread and cereal, and left to give Jamie an early morning wake-up call.

In the right scenario, she had the ammunition now to speedily summon an emotional reaction in the pit of her stomach. Thinking of Jamie being bullied or the look of sheer terror on Seamus' face as he was choking to death both inflamed her body.

She sprung up onto Jamie's window ledge and tapped on his window.

There was no reply. Just a vibrating snore that shook the very windowpanes.

She knocked again, and again, **louder** and **louder**.

Finally, he threw open the curtains and stared. He wasn't shocked or surprised. He didn't react or say anything. It was at that moment Amy realised he was still actually sleeping. She slapped the window and startled him into life. Jamie rubbed his eyes and stumbled back to his bed. Eventually, he opened the window.

"How? What?"

"I jumped."

"You jumped?" he asked looking down to the garden. "You've no ladder?"

"No. I jumped. Did you know a kangaroo rat can jump 45 times its own body length?"

Jamie gawped at the girl, with a look of admiration in his glassy eyes. "Wait, what time is it?"

"Six," replied Amy.

"Six? In the evening? You mean I've slept all day!"

"No," Amy giggled. "AM, like in the morning."

Jamie without hesitation started to close the curtains.

"Wait, Jamie! I know where Principal Thomson lives and I've got a plan."

"A plan you say," he yawned, opening the curtains and window. "And I assume you need me to execute this plan."

"Well of course. But we've got to go now!" she urged.

"Okay, just let me tell my…"

"No time," interrupted Amy. "Don't ask permission. Ask forgiveness later. It's easier." She smiled and passed him her plastic bag through the window. "Throw more cereal and bread in there. You'll soon see why."

Jamie's words rang in her head as they approached Principal Thomson's terraced house. 'You can't have superpowers and not use them.' If she did something about Principal Thomson now then perhaps school would be bearable, children would stop leaving, her abilities could remain a secret and, most importantly, her friendship with Jamie would be cemented.

The plan was simple yet brilliant. She was going to drive the cruel principal to the brink of madness and send him packing; out of the school, out of the village, and possibly, hopefully, even out of the country.

Jamie stationed himself in a neighbour's garden, opposite Principal Thomson's house. His eyes were so wide they appeared to be nothing but white as he watched Amy leap onto the principal's roof in a single bound. She hurriedly scattered the contents of the bag on the roof. Then gracefully jumped down and covered the garden with the remaining crumbs of food. The brave girl then quickly darted over to join her friend. The pair patiently waited with hope and excitement.

Eventually, the heinous principal strode out, totally unaware of what awaited him.

Principal Thomson was about to have the most peculiar of starts to his day. The roof of his house was completely concealed by roosting birds, hundreds and hundreds of them; blackbirds, rooks, magpies, sparrows, seagulls, robins, pigeons, starlings and doves.

"Is he scared of birds?" quizzed Jamie.

"Maybe. I don't know. But what do you think happens if a bird eats a lot?" she replied.

"Well, going by the pigeons in our playground, they poop a lot."

"Exactly! Look!"

The moment he stepped outside a shower of bird droppings came raining down upon him. So many colours and shades- white bird poo, grey poo, black poo, and even some purple poo from pigeons who had been eating blueberries found in the cereal.

His every step was under the cover of a moving squawking flapping cloud.

For the on-looking duo, it took all their strength to contain the giggles caught in their throat.

The principal retreated swiftly back inside and fetched an umbrella to shield himself. This didn't deter the birds. The runny poo kept falling from the sky, completely circling the petrified man, who cowered under the umbrella and made a run for his car.

Once the car door had slammed and the engine purred off down the road, Amy and Jamie fell about with laughter. Clutching their bellies, they rolled about for so long that they were nearly late for school.

9
Worth It?

The bird poo plan appeared to have worked. Tuesday morning was quiet and uneventful. And more importantly, Principal Thomson had yet to make an appearance. Miss Quinn as usual was engrossed in her silver laptop. Occasionally she banged her desk in frustration, startling the class and making them jump. But then swiftly distributed treats as a means of apology. The room was constantly filled with the hum of chatter and munching.

"Here you go children," she announced, meandering between the desks. "Some leftover cookies, waste not want not." The grinning teacher tottered around the room dispatching cookies from a plastic tub before stopping at Amy's desk. "Ahh Miss Cupples, our resident animal expert, here's a few extra for yourself." She winked and returned to her table and laptop.

Amy flashed a forced smile, but the moment Miss Quinn turned she was already on her feet and striding towards the bin.

"I don't think so," snapped Conor Phillips, as he swiped the cookies from her hand and threw them into his pocket. Chuckling he returned to his seat but not before he ripped the baked goods from Jamie too, and threw the whole thing into his mouth.

"Who cares," said Jamie defiantly. He reached into his bag and produced a multipack of Milky Way bars. Amy took one and as quietly as possible unwrapped it below her desk.

"What's his problem?" she asked, with a mouthful of chocolate.

Jamie turned to her, "Conor's a bully, always has been. He's as bad as Principal Thomson if you ask me. Perhaps they went to the same bullying school."

"Yeah, well he's just done us a favour," Amy chuckled. "I'm pretty certain that Principal Thomson has been doing something to those cookies. I don't think they are from the parents at all. He brought them in, and I saw loads of them in his house."

"Doing something? You mean like poisoning us?"

Amy wore a serious look on her face as she replied. "He must be. Notice how when he's given some cookies, he just puts them in his pocket. Never eats them."

No sooner was his name mentioned than the muscular man marched into the room and blew his whistle- loud, hard, and way too long. He clearly had an enormous lung capacity for the high pitch tone went on and on and on. The children abruptly ceased their conversations and doodling, to stick their fingers in their ears. Miss Quinn rolled her eyes and sighed; loud and deliberate.

He had forgone his usual call of 'settle down' for a deathly stare that he burned into each one of the fourteen pupils. Instantly the class was muted.

"Good morning, Principal Thomson," chirped Miss Quinn with a smile that almost cracked her face. "To what do we owe the pleasure."

The principal didn't say a word. Instead, he paced the length of the room, his whistle still in his mouth. The tension hung in the air like an over-inflated balloon on the verge of popping. And then Amy bravely, or perhaps foolishly, pushed a pin forward.

"Sir, a little birdie told me, you've won lots of medals. What did you compete in?"

Jamie gasped. The class all leaned forward with sustained focus and wide eyes.

But Principal Thomson still didn't respond. He spat out his whistle which thumped against his hard chest and narrowed his eyes on the red-haired child before him.

The man mountain turned to the seated Miss Quinn and began speaking to her in hushed tones.

The noise level in the classroom soon began to rise again and chatting resumed.

Amy and Jamie were deflated. They slumped in their chairs and shook their heads. Their antics had only served in making the principal quieter but somehow more threatening. Then the dread of what he may do next began to mount.

Behind them, the children fell silent. Amy shifted uneasily in her seat. She whipped her ponytail over her shoulder, just in case, and stroked it as it fell down the front of her chest.

SMACK!

"Ha!" Conor Phillips nearly choked. "Bulls-eye!"

"Settle down!" barked the principal. "Manners!"

Amy slowly reached to the back of her head and felt a little drenched ball of paper. She delicately plucked it from her hair and flicked it to the ground.

The giggling was suppressed, and an intrigued silence befell the class.

SMACK!

Amy didn't react this time. The little bullet sat perched in her hair.

SMACK! ## SMACK! # SMACK!

The classroom erupted with laughter, but Amy didn't move. She stared straight ahead, motionless and focused.

"Don't react," whispered Jamie. "Why don't you name the emotion, then do the opposite? Just don't reveal an ability. You'll get him back."

"Oh, I'll get him all right," she replied, with clenched fists.

Amy could hear Conor busily tearing up paper, chewing it, and making saliva-covered balls to launch at the back of her head. So focused was he on his preparation, that Conor failed to see Principal Thomson take up a position at the front of the room to settle the class, and that was his first mistake.

He loaded his mouth with a little spitball. Placed his weapon between his lips, took aim, and then unleashed the gooey bullet with a ferocious emptying of his lungs. But he hadn't counted on Amy's clever plan, and that was his second mistake. She had drawn him in. Made him confident, cocky even, then took full advantage of his arrogance. She ducked, just in the nick of time and as the spitball whooshed past her ear it headed straight for the principal. **SMACK!**

Conor's heart thumped hard and echoed around the silent room. A hundred excuses formed in his head, but they all died before they could reach his lips.

He began to stutter but said no particular words, just sounds.

Principal Thomson casually walked toward the trembling blonde boy. He didn't wipe the spitball from his face. Instead, it remained stuck high on his cheek just below his left eye.

He loomed over Conor's desk. "Mr Phillips, again. This will be the last time you and I have a run-in. Mark my words…the….last….time!" He ever so slowly removed the offending spitball from his face and placed it on the desk and turned to leave.

Conor was white and panting frantically. His wide eyes darted around the room looking for help, support, comfort; anything. But everyone avoided his gaze.

"Ah Principal Thomson, before you leave. A few cookies perhaps," offered Miss Quinn. "Goodness knows we need to treat ourselves or we'd never get through a school day. Am I right?"

Without a word, the principal snatched a handful from the tub and left the dumbfounded class in peace.

10
One Sick Bully

The playground activities were significantly more boisterous and louder than usual. Principal Thomson had abandoned his usual duties of patrol and instead only offered the occasional knock of the window in between his look to the skies. The satisfied grin on Amy's face was making her cheeks sore. And Jamie even parted with half of his second bag of crisps to guarantee to keep the principal at bay. After crushing the crisps, he scattered them next to the doors, drawing in the pesky pigeons.

When the bell rang and the children filed back inside, the principal was hovering next to the door awaiting their return. His left eye was twitching, he was foaming at the mouth and his usual gravelly voice was thin and high-pitched. He was clearly on a mission to make up for the lost time. A hush immediately descended upon the corridors. Even the teachers quickly scampered into their classrooms.

Jamie flinched and leapt into Amy as a giant hand reached over his head. The enormous grip swallowed Conor's shoulder whole.

"You're not looking too sharp, Mr Phillips," Principal Thomson rasped. "If you get any worse. Please have Miss Quinn bring you to me. I'll see that you're taken care of." With a smile, the terrifying man released the pale sweaty boy from his grasp and strutted away.

Amy couldn't help shifting uneasily in her chair. Of course, she detested Conor. But another child was off school, it was becoming ridiculous. *How was Principal Thomson doing it? Why was he doing it?*

"Miss," screeched Conor. **"Miss, I need to…."** Without waiting for her response, the blonde-haired boy covered his mouth and bolted for the door, tiny bits of vomit escaping through his fingers.

Miss Quinn exploded up from her chair like she'd been electrocuted and gave chase. "Read on," she yelled over her shoulder. "I shouldn't be long." Her tapping high heels echoed down the corridor like a galloping horse on a cobbled stone street.

Amy, wide-eyed, turned to Jamie and mouthed, "That's seven now!"

"Eight if you include old Mrs Gallen?" Jamie replied solemnly.

Amy just shook her head and tutted. She began scanning the room and the oblivious children surrounding her. Who would be next? The minutes ticked by slowly; particularly for Jamie who was dying to use the toilet but wouldn't dare leave the classroom without permission. The remaining pupils chatted as the lunch bell came and went. Nobody made the first move. All the intrigued eyes bounced around the room and heads motioned towards the door, egging someone to lead the way.

Jamie, nearly blue in the face, leapt from his seat and raced to the door. The rest all followed suit.

After lunch, Miss Quinn returned to her position behind her laptop. She threw out textbooks, wrote a page number on the whiteboard and as per usual paid the children little attention. Instead, she resumed frantically typing away on her keyboard, all the while looking especially happy.

Amy and Jamie busied themselves trying to devise a plan. Whatever Principal Thomson was up to they needed to put an end to it, sharpish. As they sketched ideas and wrote lists, Amy fought against the rage already swelling inside her. The moments of injustice spun around her head like a carousel. She was gaining confidence; a belief she could call upon a power if required.

The three o'clock home time bell was greeted with a collective sigh of relief. Miss Quinn herself was out of the room before the children had even packed up.

"So, we hit Thomson's house first. While he's still at school," confirmed Amy.

"Okay," Jamie agreed, reluctantly. A quiver in his voice.

"It'll be fine. Come on!"

As the pair were carried towards the school gates by the exiting mob, they heard an unusual remark which piqued their curiosity.

"Is that your boyfriend, Miss?"

Arm in arm Miss Quinn and Principal Thomson were stumbling towards the school car park. The large principal glared in the direction of the yelled comment before forcing a wry smile. They both climbed into a little green car and sped off.

"Her too!" exclaimed Jamie. "He's done it to her too. That's why she ran out of the classroom before us. She's sick. What on earth is he doing?"

"We're gonna find out," Amy replied, already marching towards the exit.

*

"Look, Amy, no car," said Jamie as they approached the principal's house.

"Perfect. Perhaps he's not here yet. Maybe stopped off somewhere. Come on, we can sneak in before he comes back."

Jamie popped some gum into his mouth and forced a smile, "I knew you'd say that."

75

"Check the back door and windows, I'll do the front. If you find anything whistle."

The brave duo went their separate ways in search of a way to get inside. The curtains were drawn allowing no view in, and, besides the smell of bird poo behind her, the front of the house didn't offer a sniff of hope. Sensibly the windows were shut keeping out the odour and the red front door was locked.

Moments later Jamie flew past Amy whistling like a steam train. She'd never seen him move so quickly before. Chin up, back straight and knees high he motored down the street screaming, **"He's coming! He's coming!"**

Amy quickly tailed it after her friend and caught him just yards down the street, clinging to a wall, and panting desperately. His eyes were wide and his voice trembling, "Quick, he's coming," he announced before taking off again.

"Is he in? Is it Thomson?" she yelled after him.

Jamie didn't run much further. A few more yards along he sat resting against another wall, gasping for air.

"Did he see you, what happened? Was he there?" rushed Amy as she crouched down.

Jamie didn't reply. He was curled into a ball and shaking. Amy paused, befuddled. He finally emerged to point back down the road from where he came. His eyes were so big, all that could be seen were the whites. His breath was loud, short and uncontrollable. Amy herself froze. Her heart leapt into her throat as an enormous shadow loomed over the two shaking friends.

She took a long deep breath in through her nose making her nostrils flap then tentatively turned around to face the owner of the threatening shadow. Jamie flung himself behind her for protection.

Amy's giggle was not one of comfort to her friend. It seemed to make him only more nervous. He was grabbing her shoulders so tightly that Amy was convinced he may draw blood.

"Relax," she pleaded. "It's only Seamus. He's a friendly big dog."

"Big dog? Big dog?!" Jamie repeated, exasperated. "That's no big dog. That's a horse, or a hairy dinosaur or something. That's no dog."

Amy put her hand out for Seamus to sniff. The large dog's tail immediately began wagging, sending a burst of cool air across Amy's face, and pushing her red hair into Jamie's face.

Jamie nervously stepped out and approached the dog. He cautiously patted the tan gentle giant before stepping back behind Amy again. "Fair enough, you've made friends with Thomson's guard dog. But there's no way in."

"There's always a way in," grinned Amy.

As she hoped, like before, a window was still ajar at the back of the house. Amy, in a single bound, scaled the height of the house and darted through the house to let Jamie in.

"No, no. I'll keep a lookout," he suggested. "Go see what you can find."

There was nothing though. None of the missing children or teachers. No clues. No hints, tips or evidence, nothing.

"Maybe he takes them somewhere else," ventured Amy. "We'll have to follow him tomorrow when he takes his next victim. Are you okay with that?"

"Yeah, yeah, of course, whatever," said Jamie, who was too busy feeding Seamus crisps from his schoolbag to listen. "One for you, one for me. Good dog."

11
Two Weeks

The next morning Amy and Jamie arrived at school bright, early, and eager. Time was running out, as well as the number of children. But as they approached the building, they saw the little green car already squatting in the car park. However, something even more alarming greeted them inside.

A delicious smell of warm chocolate brownies wafted out of the classroom. Even children not in Amy's class were caught drifting in and hoping to avail themselves of the irresistible gooey treat.

"Wait! What? It can't be!" exclaimed Jamie, rooted to the spot.

"It was her?" exclaimed Amy, looking wide-eyed and confused.

They staggered towards their table and fell into their seats. Miss Quinn was proudly balancing a tray of brownies in one hand as she shooed out visiting children and closed the door.

"A fresh batch, children," she proclaimed. "Baked only this morning. Come and get them while they're hot."

"I suppose it makes more sense," suggested Jamie.

"Really?" replied Amy, furrowing her brow.

"Well, Principal Thomson's always been evil. Like for years," he replied. "Why would he suddenly start getting rid of pupils? But Miss Quinn arrived, and it all began. But hey, at least she's only here for two weeks."

"Two weeks!" screeched Amy, a little too loudly. Miss Quinn whipped her head around and smiled across the room at the girl. "My parents! They're away for two weeks."

"You don't think she's done something to them?"

"I do," she gulped. "It's too much of a coincidence. And I haven't even heard from them. I know they would have phoned to check on me. Especially since they know I hate staying at my uncle Jack's house." Her heart thumped against her chest and her whole body began to shake.

"It's just an opinion, it's just an opinion," she recited over and over.

"What is?" probed Jamie. "What are you doing? Is this another technique to control emotions?"

"Yeah. Opinions hold no weight and we shouldn't let them impact us. Only facts are true."

Jamie patted her shoulder, "Look don't worry. If it is a fact, we'll follow her home and rescue them. We'll rescue them all."

"And I've two left," announced Miss Quinn. "Ah Amy, Jamie, come on ahead."

Amy shook her head violently. "No thank you, Miss."

"Not hungry?" enquired the teacher. "How about you, Jamie? They are sickeningly good." The teacher began meandering menacingly between the desks all the while never taking her eyes off Amy.

"No, he doesn't want one either, Miss," replied Amy. Jamie stared longingly at the brownie and elbowed Amy.

"I'll take them, Miss," bellowed a dark-haired girl from the rear of the room.

"Don't be silly," purred Miss Quinn. "I won't see anybody left out. Especially not you two. Here you go." She delicately placed the two chocolate treats onto the desk and then twirled on her high heels. "Right, page thirty-six today. No interruptions. I've my own work to do." She plopped herself in front of her laptop and hid from the class behind the screen.

"No! Don't!" said Amy, snapping the brownie from Jamie's grasp. "Can't you see what she's doing?" Amy marched towards the bin; her arm outstretched.

"I'll take those," said the dark-haired girl, snatching the brownies from her.

"But those..." started Amy.

"Are mine," interjected the girl, laughing.

A chorus of giggles filled the classroom. Amy could feel her very fingertips tingle with fury. "Okay, suit yourself."

Jamie wiped the drool away from the corner of his mouth. "So, she's the one poisoning us!" he stated as Amy bounced back into her seat.

"Exactly, it hasn't been Principal Thomson. It never was."

"But why? What's she up to?"

"I don't know, but we need to find out."

Like waiting for Christmas morning to arrive, the time passed painfully slow. Amy spent her entire morning watching the hands of the clock tick by and tortured herself with images of what Miss Quinn could be doing with her parents.

It didn't take long for another victim to fall ill. And unsurprisingly it was the dark-haired girl who had scoffed three times as many brownies as the rest of the class. Still, despite vomiting, she looked pleased to be getting out of class.

"Heads down, not a peep. I shan't be long. I've just to take care of…" the teacher paused.

"Niamh," stated the girl.

"Of course. Right, let's go."

Amy slipped out of her seat with a mischievous glint in her eyes and a devilish grin on her face. "Stay here," she said to Jamie, who was already rising from his chair too.

Amy bolted to the nearest girls' toilet. Her body was still flooded with worry. *Where are Mum and Dad? Would Miss Quinn be off with Jamie next?* She quickly locked herself in a cubicle and removed her uniform. But this time she was prepared. Throughout her entire previous invisible escapade, she was fearful of suddenly losing her ability and becoming visible. *Could you imagine! How embarrassing!* Below her uniform, she had a sequinned dress that she had once seen her mum wear. Amy recalled that her Mum looked like a walking mirror or even a giant disco ball. It was perfect. Amy would move with such speed and stealth that anyone who thought they saw something would just as quickly dismiss it as a reflection or a trick of the light. She hung her uniform on the back of the door and put her shoes behind the cistern, then exited completely and utterly invisible. She watched herself stroll past the rows of mirrors, her heart still thumping feverishly at the remarkable ability she possessed. *You can do this!*

Despite being virtually undetectable to the human eye, the same could not be said for the human ear so she ever so quietly scurried through the corridors in search of Miss Quinn and Niamh.

She had a particularly tense moment when she passed a line of Year Threes going to the PE hall. Amy carelessly stepped on a stray sharpener and unwillingly released a little yelp. She froze, the line froze, and every one of the tiny pupils stared directly at her, before shrugging their shoulders and moving on.

Amy managed to catch the fiendish teacher just as she approached the secretary's office. "Yeah another one," remarked Miss Quinn. "Could I have Niamh's number please?" She then nonchalantly sauntered out of the school with her next victim in tow.

Why is she leaving the school with a pupil? Isn't anyone going to stop her?

Amy followed the pair to the teacher's little green car. Niamh by now was yellow and unsteady on her feet. Her mouth was hanging open and her eyes looked lazy. The petit teacher placed the pupil into the back seat and then withdrew her mobile phone.

"Ah, Niamh's mother I presume. Miss Quinn here from Barrack Street Primary. I have some fantastic news. Your wonderful daughter has been selected to represent the school in a forthcoming school quiz. This does mean she will be away for a few days….. Oh no no. There's no need. The school will provide everything, at no expense to you. It is short notice I understand, but that's how these things work…..

I assure you she will be perfectly fine and will be home in a matter of days, hopefully with a winning medal," she laughed. "Okay, bye for now."

What is she doing? Amy could only watch as the little car whisked Niamh off. She turned and marched back into school, more determined than ever to do something about it.

12
Shoelaces

A ruckus spilling out of her classroom stopped Amy dead in her tracks. She had neglected her careful approach to keeping quiet and ploughed right into the room. The door swung open and the whole class froze. They waited for someone to enter, but no one did. Still invisible, Amy was aghast at the sight before her. Instant anger coursed through her so violently she was trembling. The sound of her grinding teeth could even be heard over the clatter of teasing she witnessed.

Jamie, tearful and sweaty, was chasing his pencil case that a group of six children were tossing around. The smiling faces and hoots of laughter would have you believe the class were having fun, but they weren't, not all of them.

Mrs Jennings came storming into the room, her floating long dress spinning like a tornado. She spoke in harsh clipped tones, "Who on earth do you think you are? Get into your seats now! How rude! How disrespectful! I should never hear this class above my own. For goodness sake, you're at the opposite end of the corridor. If I hear so much as a child breathing heavily, every one of you will be in detention." She kept a silent intense watch as all the pupils returned to their seats. "And do not dare leave your seat, for anything!"

Even as Mrs Jennings's last sentence still hung in the air, it gave Amy an idea. A revengeful idea. Very cautiously the invisible girl crept from table to table and began tying the shoelace of all six bullies to the leg of their table.

As she headed for the toilet again to get changed, she whispered into her friend's ear, "Forget about them, Jamie. They aren't worth it." She lifted the pencil case and set it on his table.

Of course, to Jamie the red pencil case floated, he was hearing voices and he hadn't breathed in a good two minutes. He reached a quaking hand out in front of him tentatively. But Amy was already gone.

He nearly fell off his seat when she returned. "Invisible?" he croaked. "Did you? When I was?" he stuttered.

"I did," whispered Amy. "Just another superpower."

"Ahhh, the ultimate superpower I think you will find," Jamie smiled. "So, Miss Quinn, what happened?"

"Well, she's definitely the one making us sick. But she's not taking them home. I think she might be taking them all to her place."

"To do what?"

"I've no idea," gulped Amy.

BRRINNNGGGG

THUMP THUMP **THUMP**

Amy and Jamie squealed with laughter as everyone around them fell to the floor.

"I take it that was *your* doing?" quizzed Jamie. Already knowing the answer, he didn't wait for a reply. "Genius. Just genius!"

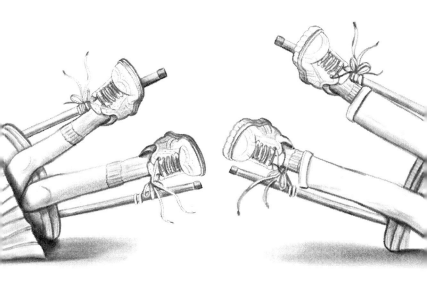

*

To call Miss Quinn a teacher is to use the term very loosely. Sure, she stood at the front of the room and wrote the odd instruction on the whiteboard, but she did no actual teaching. Her entire school day was spent on her laptop. And ever since she managed to rid the school of Principal Thomson, which of course some children were thrilled about, she had changed. Even her sweet perfume became suffocating, wafting up the nostrils of all twelve pupils, tingeing the hairs. Her threatening glares, snappy remarks and frustration with any child were growing by the minute.

She had returned after lunch, minus Niamh of course, and busied herself on a new laptop. A laptop computer that Amy recognised instantly, sending a shudder down her spine.

Miss Quinn gently placed the new laptop on her desk, swapping it with her own and transferring all the wires, all the while a smile grew wider and wider upon her face, practically reaching one ear to the other.

A pain in her stomach suggested to Amy something more serious was on the horizon. As she stared at the black laptop covered in animal stickers she panicked, *what did Miss Quinn do to my parents?*

"What's wrong?" asked Jamie, seeing Amy's pale complexion and fingertips tapping the desk.

"Look," she replied nodding towards Miss Quinn. "That's my parent's laptop. It's an old one they used for work."

"Do you think she got it when she took your parents?"

"Well, I do now," Amy replied, biting her bottom lip.

"Your little jolly is over," Miss Quinn purred, with a hint of menace in her voice. "I've work to do. Silence everyone!" She scowled over the laptop screen forcing the class to drop silent and their eyes to quickly fall upon their books.

The computer started up and rang out its little opening jiggle. It was the only sound in the classroom. Amy watched on anxiously with bated breath. The smile upon her teacher's face grew wider still, before abruptly vanishing. She smashed the desk with her two fists in anger, startling the entire class. **"No! No! No!"** she yelled. She began tapping and clicking keys furiously. **'BANG!'** She smashed the tabletop again sending the remote control for the projector tumbling to the ground. The projector turned on and oblivious to the teacher, the entire class, well those who dared to look, could see the computer screen behind Miss Quinn in 100-inch colourful glory.

Amy edged closer, precariously balancing her seat on two legs. Her feet were feverously tapping as her knees knocked uncontrollably.

"Keep it down," drawled the teacher. She folded the screen down slightly to survey the room. Her gaze fixed on Amy before her eyes twinkled and she frantically began typing.

-**Cupples**. Incorrect password. 9 attempts remaining.

-**AmyCupples.** Incorrect password. 8 attempts remaining.

-**Snakes**. Incorrect password. 7 attempts remaining.

Every unsuccessful attempt was marked with an angry thumping upon her desk.

-**Medicine.** Incorrect password. 6 attempts remaining.

-**OurlittleAmy.** Incorrect password. 5 attempts remaining

Amy took a long deep breath, held it and cautiously approached the teacher's desk. She kept her head down and tried not to look at the screen behind Miss Quinn. "Need some help Miss?" she offered. "I'm good on computers."

Miss Quinn froze and threw Amy a deathly stare. She didn't speak, instead focused on the child before her whilst bouncing her tongue pensively between her top and bottom lip. Suddenly she flashed her teeth like a shark prepped for an attack, "Oh don't worry you've helped."

Amy stumbled as she backed away from the sinister gaze. She gulped, it was hard and dry. Fear had taken hold. Like a slippery eel wriggling around her body, sliding over her stomach, head and heart. And she couldn't get a grip of it. She couldn't do anything. She cowered back into her desk and stared hopelessly at the screen.

-RedheadAmy **DING!** Access granted.

A family photo of Amy, Mum and Dad at the beach filled the screen. Gazing upon it, a butterfly somersaulted in Amy's stomach as Miss Quinn opened a folder. The screen title read- 'Cupples and associate - Disease Cure Research'. A thousand questions flooded Amy's mind. None of which she could answer. *What did this mean? Was it her parent's work? Why would Miss Quinn steal the laptop?*

"Here Miss, what's that? Is that because she's new in school or something?" yelled a small girl in the front row with a squeaky voice. She pointed to the presentation illuminated on the screen.

Miss Quinn turned her head around. The slow movements only added to the tense situation. She deliberately remained fixed upon Amy as she reached for the little remote control, flicked off the screen and smirked.

13
White Lab Coat

When you have a superpower, particularly that of invisibility, following someone is easy. Even following someone in a car isn't much trouble when you can run faster than the speeding car itself. The trouble was, that at the end of the school day, Amy had to do both. And she had learnt that moving around barefooted can be painful. So, when three o'clock came, she darted to the toilets, threw her detested brown uniform in her schoolbag and chased Miss Quinn's car – on foot; in trainers, and donning her Mum's reflective disco dress.

Amy didn't have time to concern herself with being quiet or avoid bumping into pupils leaving school. In all the chaos of the mass exit, she managed to reach the main road quickly and was in hot pursuit of the little green car. Unsurprisingly, a pair of trainers running, floating in the air, did bring about some peculiar looks. But then they were moving at such speeds that many of the witnesses dismissed them instantly as a cat or something in the wind.

Miss Quinn didn't live far from the school. *That's how she managed to accompany the missing pupils to her home and still be back in school in a short period of time,* thought Amy. She followed the deceitful teacher to her front door and watched her go in. The house didn't look like anything especially unique. Not a lair, no concealed entrances and not somewhere you'd imagine kidnapped people would be taken. But maybe, thought Amy, that was Miss Quinn's cleverness, to hide in plain sight.

With Jamie still awaiting her return, she headed back to school and changed before the duo bravely ventured towards Miss Quinn's house together.

"Slowdown will ya," panted Jamie. "You're gonna give me a heart attack." He stopped and withdrew an energy drink from his bag. "Knew I'd need this. Want some?"

"No, no, come on. God knows what she's doing!"

"Wait, you need to think about this. We need a plan. This is the same woman who has kidnapped children from school, your parents too. She won't think twice about hurting two more kids who land in her house."

Amy slowed her pace. A cloud of fear reigned over her, washing away her anger. He was right. This needed to be played carefully.

In tandem, they stealthily crept to the downstairs window of Miss Quinn's two-storey terrace house. Ever so cautiously Amy raised her eyes above the sill and dared to peek in. With a sweaty hand, she yanked Jamie up. They scanned the room.

"She's disgusting," whispered Jamie. "That's worse than my brother's room."

Dirty dishes were resting on every available surface, empty Pot Noodle cartons were built up like the leaning tower of Pisa and clothes were piled in an open suitcase; some had even made a break towards the kitchen and the washing machine. The house wasn't a home. It was like a hotel room, with a guest who didn't plan on staying.

"Which power will we use? Go invisible maybe. Sneak in and see what's what," suggested Jamie, wiping his forehead with the back of his sleeve.

"We need to check first, wait up there." Amy directed Jamie to the other end of the street.

She cautiously approached the front door, brushed her hair away from her face, took a deep breath and pushed the doorbell. Miss Quinn could be heard angrily thundering through the house and grunting towards the door. Amy took off. Running so quickly it stung her eyes. She joined Jamie who was nonchalantly perched on a wall, his feet dangling inches from the pavement and his eyes eager. A safe distance away they watched as Miss Quinn stepped out of her house.

Simultaneously they gasped and elbowed each other. Miss Quinn didn't look like the teacher from school. Not while wearing a long white lab coat, rubber gloves and goggles around her neck. She wore a serious scowl upon her face and held in one clenched fist a handful of vibrant red hair. The annoyed woman marched from side to side before stomping back inside and slamming the door.

"Well at least we know she's home," said Jamie, jumping off the wall and falling to his knees. He used his pudgy hands to wipe his trousers before standing up.

"Yeah, but didn't you notice something?"

"Her scientist outfit?" offered Jamie.

"Well, yes, but in her hand. She had my hair clippings! Remember the ones Conor cut off in class?"

"This is just getting weird," mused Jamie. "No bother to you though, use your speed, and your strength. Throw her out and rescue your parents. Easy."

If only it were that easy, thought Amy.

"I can't," she replied.

"You can't?"

"I can't," confirmed Amy, jumping down to stand next to her friend. She placed a hand on his shoulder. "Think about it. She's got the upper hand. If we try anything, she'll just hurt my parents and the others."

"Yeah but who's to say she hasn't already," interjected Jamie.

Amy gulped and began twisting her hair around her fingers.

"I know," she blurted. "We'll wait, the moment she's out, then we're in!" She grabbed her friend by his school bag and hauled him behind a wall with a perfect view of Miss Quinn's house.

The night sky soon crept over the street and the orange glow from the lamp posts only added to the dreaded scene. Jamie, so determined to help his friend, skipped dinner and replaced it with three visits to the local shop while Amy remained on the lookout. The three Mars bars and two bags of popcorn did little to silence either rumbling tummy.

Just as Amy considered plucking up the courage to face the vile teacher, Miss Quinn finally made an appearance. With her handbag tucked under her arm, she hopped into her car and sped off. The two friends didn't hang about. They darted over to the house immediately.

Amy's beating heart shook her whole body. She was jittery, hopping from foot to foot, swinging between fear and excitement.

In unison, they took a deep breath and moved in.

"Do you hear that?" whispered Amy.

Jamie held his breath to silence his pounding heart. "What is it? An animal?" he suggested.

"Animals. Plural. And they sound in pain."

As they drew nearer, their short frantic breaths were drowned out by the sound of animal cries emanating from inside.

A poker hot flash of fury filled Amy's body as she threw her shoulder into the locked door. The anger turned her cheeks crimson as the door yielded and burst open with a clatter.

The house smelled even worse than it looked. She had no pride in her home, a bit like her teaching approach. But in the distance, a faint smell of disinfectant hung in the air. The pair weaved their way through the mess and into the kitchen towards the clinically clean smell. The strong aroma stung the eyes.

"What's that?" asked Jamie, holding his breath. "Sounds like an elephant."

"An African elephant to be exact," added Amy.

"Is that a lion I can hear too, an angry lion?" Jamie was already backing away.

"It's a tiger in fact," Amy corrected. "Lions, tigers, jaguars and leopards are the only cats that can roar. But that was certainly a tiger, about ten years old too if I'm not mistaken."

Jamie smiled at Amy's insightful knowledge. "It sounds like a zoo. Glad we're not going down there."

Amy just stared at her friend without blinking.

"We're going down there, aren't we?" asked Jamie, already fearing he knew the answer.

"We've got to!"

Behind the kitchen, a narrow corridor lead to another room from where the cacophony of sounds stemmed. The friends advanced, quick-footed with caution.

Amy pulled on the handle of the steel door. It remained steady, solid and impenetrable.

"Ah would you look at that, the door's locked," announced Jamie. "Guess we'll have to go then."

Amy raised her eyebrows and smirked. "Can't you hear that?" she asked.

"I can! I can hear they all sound big and angry."

"No, listen. Someone is crying for help."

Jamie pressed his ear to the cold metal door. "The only cries you'll be hearing are mine. It's just animals in there. Now come on. The door is locked for a reason. For safety, our safety."

Amy studied the door before her, the double locks and electronic keypad that allows entry. "Who has this much security on a single door? There must be something in there that she doesn't want anyone to see."

"And you think it could be your parents."

"Exactly!"

"Okay then, no point coming this far for nothing," said Jamie, puffing out his chest. "Use those powers of yours again."

"Step aside."

Amy smiled before thundering towards the door. She drop-kicked it with the soles of her feet and sent the door crashing to the ground. Jamie quickly jumped into the girl's shadow as they slowly entered.

14
Animals and Cages

The room was long and narrow. To the rear was another door. It stood solid and secure, covered with a sheet of thick shiny metal, which appeared to prevent access or entry. On the right side of the room was a solitary window and a long worktop laden with beakers, textbooks and test tubes. On the opposing side of the room were cages three high and stretching the length of the room. Around half of the cages were covered with a blanket that concealed only the appearance of the animal within but certainly not the sounds. The moment the door opened the room erupted.

Amy raced straight towards the wall of cages whilst Jamie remained hugging the doorframe. Eventually, he slid over to the worktop, drawn in by something familiar.

"You were right," Jamie said. "Look-"

Amy turned and joined him to study the contents of the worktop. "Yeah I know, that's my parents' laptop."

"No, I mean that," he replied, pointing towards a microscope.

The intrigued girl's eyes fell upon a very professional and expensive-looking microscope.

Nothing like the little dinky one she received for Christmas when she was seven. But more fascinating was the subject matter being examined. Her very own shiny red hair was delicately positioned under the lens.

"What has she been doing with it?"

"I've no idea," replied Amy, moving in closer to look through the microscope.

Jamie timidly stepped towards the cages. He stretched out a hand and considered revealing the occupant behind each curtain but thought better of it when he heard a collection of screeches, howls, snorts and grunts.

"Calm down," he yelled, backing away. **"We're here to help."**

They did as he requested. Silence fell over the room. Amy popped up and returned her focus to the cages and the labels above them.

"Did they just understand me?" gulped Jamie.

"I think so," smiled Amy. "They should do though, look at the labels." She walked the length of the cages pointing at the little boards above each one containing a name in perfect handwriting. "Paul, Niamh, Conor…"

"Wait!" interrupted Jamie. "She's keeping them in cages. What's all the animal noise about?"

Amy drew back the black curtain covering Conor's cage and stole a glance inside. "He's a little horse."

"A little hoarse? Give him a soother then to suck on, that'll help his throat," snorted Jamie. "Why did he go home sick? Typical, he just wanted out of school I bet."

"No," replied Amy, throwing the curtain over the top of the cage. "He's actually a little horse!"

Jamie's mouth was stretched wide prepared to release an ear-piercing scream, but nothing but a dry splutter escaped.

Amy moved over to her friend and whispered to him, "I think the animals *are* the people she has kidnapped."

"The animals are the people she kidnapped?" repeated Jamie incredulously.

Amy surveyed the trapped victims before her. Her bright eyes were pulled towards two cages, labelled adult male and an adult female. "Mum, Dad," she croaked. Her heart leapt into her throat preventing her from speaking. She didn't move either. The shock had rooted her heavy feet to the floor.

"But how? I don't understand." Jamie puffed out his red cheeks and neared the caged animals. "At least they look happy to.....what's that smell?" He stopped, lifted his nose to the air and drew in a long deep sniff. "Pizza! Pepperoni and pineapple pizza!"

"She's back!" whispered Amy, hearing the front door slam closed.

Jamie began sweating profusely as he watched Amy race around the cages returning the curtains over each.

"Get in!" she barked. **"Get in quickly!"** Amy held a cage door open.

"Are you mad?" he said abruptly.

"Well, it's up to you. Or maybe you'd rather she turned you into an animal too."

Jamie didn't reply. In a flash, he fell to his knees and crawled into the cage. Amy felt the fearful sweat on the back of his jumper as she edged him into the cage. She quickly closed the door and dropped the curtain.

The trapped and mistreated animals were enough to spark anger in her chest. When she thought of the trapped and mistreated, Jamie the anger was inflamed. As the warm itch spread through her body, she looked for somewhere to hide her uniform.

To the rear of the room, she discovered a basket filled with school uniforms. The undeniable horrible brown uniform of Barrack Street Primary. Of course, she thought, the caged pupils, their uniforms. She tossed hers on top of the pile, held her breath and retreated into the corner of the room now invisible.

15
Breaking Doors

Amy's wait was made even more nervous when Miss Quinn stomped into the room. Red-faced and seething, the woman's beady dark eyes traced the room and the tip of her tongue circled her tight lips.

She tossed a pizza box onto the worktop and stood resolutely in the centre of the room, taking long deep breaths. As Amy stared on, she considered if fury had clogged her teacher's ears for the animals were going wild and she didn't react. Jamie's cage was violently shaking as he sobbed.

Amy's head swirled with ideas. *Should she attack? Use her powers and throw the cruel teacher in a cage. But then how would she get answers? How could she turn everyone back into a human?*

The teacher's head began to bob up and down. *Was she counting the cages? Did she notice the extra tenant?* Slowly the teacher approached the rows of cages and began flicking the curtains menacingly. Then starting on the top row, she moved along from right to left, whipping back any curtain she met and snarling at the animal inside. On each occasion, she met an empty cage she ran her long fingernails along the bars sounding out a haunting count down until Jamie was discovered. The first row was complete.

Now the second row. Amy needed to act fast and do something. Otherwise, Jamie was done for the moment Miss Quinn reached the third, final and lowest row of cages.

Without care for noise or a second to spare the invisible girl bolted through the lab, down the corridor and towards the front door. Barely hanging on its hinges, she flung it open and frantically rang the doorbell over and over and over. The incessant chime rang out and summoned the infuriated teacher. Amy darted back in the opposite direction, careful to avoid Miss Quinn as she did so. Without a moment to spare, she threw on her uniform, revealed herself and opened Jamie's cage.

"Quick, quick, come on!"

Jamie quickly scuttled out, and still, on his knees, he crawled towards the silver door to the rear. "There's no handle!" he screeched. "We're trapped!"

But Amy didn't notice the panic in her friend's voice. She was much too busy freeing the pair of animals labelled as adults. First was a tiny little grey mouse that sprung out and darted up Amy's leg, straight into her hand.

"Stop banging the door, Jamie, come here! Take that one," she instructed, pointing to a large muscular dog that despite looking pleased to be free, his flashing teeth didn't help put the boy at ease.

"No, no, no," he stammered. "I'll take that," he gestured towards the little mouse.

Amy handed him the mouse and then took a tie from the pile of uniforms. Using it as a leash she tied it around the dog. Her eyes frantically circled the fortified room for an exit. As she saw the pale look that Jamie wore, she took a deep breath and motored towards the reinforced metal-covered door.

She didn't have time to test the door's strength. As she steamed towards it, she pondered if there existed a world record for breaking down doors. She flattened the third with ease and spilt out onto a paved back garden. The duo made good their escape, but not before Jamie snatched the pizza from the worktop.

*

"Do you know that's the first argument we've had?" grinned Jamie as he swallowed the last slice of pizza.

"Yeah well I'm telling you, pineapple doesn't belong on a pizza," stated Amy, with a stern face but smiling eyes.

"Let's agree to disagree. I'll tell you what though, one thing we can agree on is that we're heroes and Miss Quinn is evil." He darted in front of Amy and began to walk backwards, face to face, "So, what now? We can't let her get away with it!"

"Who will believe us? I mean, a teacher turning people into animals," she snorted. "How? Why? I think the important thing now is to turn them back." She patted her Dad on the head and Jamie scratched the back of her mousy mum. "And obviously we have to rescue everyone else."

"So, will we go back tomorrow, when she's in school? We can bunk off and head back to her house."

"That's the last thing we should do, Jamie. That's like admitting guilt. She'll know it was us. And no doubt we'd be next. No, I think we need to go to school, just play dumb. I think I've got a plan, it'll get us into her house again."

"Was that in your plan?" Jamie asked, seeing the dog squat to relieve himself. "Ah, that's disgusting."

"Have you a bag or anything?" she asked.

"Just leave it, come on."

"No way! I hate people who don't pick up dog poo. They shouldn't own a dog."

"I've got this," replied Jamie, handing her an empty Mars bar wrapper.

Amy smiled through gritted teeth and reluctantly scooped up the little brown log into the chocolate bar wrapper.

"EEWWWwwwww! I'm gonna be sick!" cried Jamie, retching.

The tiny mouse bolted down Jamie's body and into his trouser pocket. Amy burst into a fit of laughter as she spied the tiny balls of mouse droppings in Jamie's hand.

"Hey! Where the hell have you been?"

The pair stood stationary under a streetlight as a heavy-footed person lumbered towards them. Their hearts pounded in unison. Their noses both wrinkled at the vile odour filling their hands.

"Who is it?" whispered Jamie. Amy rolled her eyes.

"Oi, Losers!"

"Deep breath," Amy whispered. "Fact or opinion?"

"Definitely an opinion," grinned Jamie.

"Exactly, I don't see any losers. Nope, can't be talking to us."

"Stop now, twerp! Where are you going?"

Amy sighed loudly and turned to face her two cousins Clare and Cleo. "I was just on my way home, actually."

"Well, *actually*, you should have been home hours ago," replied Clare.

"Not that we care like. But when we are sent out looking for you, then it becomes a problem," added Cleo, approaching with a clenched fist. "Oh would you look here, Clare, the little geeks are stuffing their faces."

Clare quickly waded in, and like her sister, spotted the 'chocolates' in Amy and Jamie's hands. 'Give us those!"

"Oh no you can't," Amy argued, in a tone that suggested she wasn't arguing at all. "Please, we just bought them in the shop," she continued in a dull monotone fashion.

Jamie knew exactly what she was doing. His shoulders were already bouncing with laughter as the sisters moved in to snatch the chocolates.

"I'll have the Mars bar," insisted Cleo. "You take his Maltesers."

"Now scram!" barked Clare.

Amy, Jamie, the mouse and the dog didn't need any more encouragement. They took off before the chocolate delights were chewed upon. As they raced away, the sound of dry gagging and yelps of pain echoed behind them. They only dared stop when they thought the twins couldn't catch up.

"What's that, Amy?" panted Jamie as he bent down to pick up something shining under the streetlight. "It fell from the dog's neck."

He studied the object before unwillingly handing it to his friend. Amy's heart sank and her shoulder slumped. "You know what this means?" Jamie asked.

Amy put the whistle around her neck. "Yeah it means the dog is Principal Thomson, and the mouse must be Mrs Gallen. They're not my parents."

"Exactly! That means she hasn't got your parents. They really must be off working for two weeks.'

Amy smiled meekly.

"Hey, you two!" yelled one of the twins in the distance. "Stay there! Take your chocolate back!"

16
Run Mouse, Run

The next morning in class Miss Quinn was red in the face, throbbing veins angry. Her eyes bulged, her fists were clenched and not a pupil dared look in her direction.

The teacher had skipped all pleasantries and was more ruthless than ever. Whatever she was up to at home with the animals and her lab, the rescue mission and escaped animals made her only more determined. Amy sat, curiously observing her and endlessly twisting the end of her ponytail around her finger. Miss Quinn pottered around the room practically force-feeding doughnuts to each of the pupils, none of whom appeared to mind.

"She wants more, needs to make up for the missing animals," Amy whispered into her friend's ear. "Remember don't eat the doughnuts!"

"I'm not a doughnut, of course not!" smiled Jamie.

Miss Quinn finally reached the pair of friends' table. She stared at them intensely before offering out a plastic tub. "Help yourself."

"No thanks, Miss," said Jamie, swiftly. "I don't like them."

"Liar! Take them, now!"

Jamie cautiously reached into the clear box and withdrew a solitary sugar-coated doughnut.

"More!" she hissed, shoving the container under his nose.

He quickly dipped another hand in and withdrew a second doughnut. He set both carefully onto his desk and forced a response, "Mmmm, thanks."

"And you Miss Cupples," the teacher purred. "Take some."

Amy reached into the box, took a doughnut and shoved it into her mouth. Jamie gasped, a little too loudly.

Miss Quinn flashed a horrid smile, drooling with evil intent. Suddenly she stooped down to look Amy in the eye. "What's that around your neck, child?"

Amy reached for Principal Thomson's whistle and hid it in a fist. "Nothing, Miss."

She knows! Amy's heart pounded so hard she thought it would break her ribs. In a panic, she reached across the table and snatched Jamie's two doughnuts. "They are delicious."

The colour drained from Jamie's face. He sat in his chair like a marble statue.

"We can't leave you out," purred Miss Quinn, returning her attention to the boy. She began delicately building a tower of sugar doughnuts on Jamie's table until it was tall enough to reach his mouth. "Don't you dare touch them, Cupples!" she cackled. "They're all for lovely, Jamie here. Go on, tuck in."

Amy needed to do something, quick! Fear was building up in her chest and threatening to escape from her mouth as a terrified scream, or worse an ability was about to be uncontrollably revealed. She needed a distraction, a fire alarm, a phone call, anything. She scoured the room frantically. Then she saw it. It was small, hairy, and moving. She reached into Jamie's bag and withdrew the rescued mouse, Mrs Gallen. She gently placed the little mouse onto the floor.

"Look Miss, **a mouse!!**" yelled another pupil.

"Where? Where's the little beast? I'll stamp him good!" hollered Miss Quinn, suddenly swinging on her heels and looking in the direction of all the pointing fingers. "Hey, I know that mouse!"

"I saw it run behind the bookshelf," Amy yelled over the buzzing classroom of excitement. "Listen."

"Shut up you slugs!" screeched the teacher. The class fell silent.

Miss Quinn tiptoed towards the bookshelf, held her breath and listened intently. "I can hear it. I can hear it rustling! But not for long!" She darted to the store cupboard and returned with a broom. "Escape from me will you! Ha!"

Creeping over to the bookshelf, she wore a steely-eyed look of focus. She rocked the bookshelf right then left to its tipping point and watched as the tiny grey mouse bolted out in fear. She jumped back, startled by the speed of the creature. The chase was on.

The mouse hugged the walls with the teacher in pursuit. It weaved around the tables, between two bins, behind the radiator, under Miss Quinn's desk and behind the projector screen. In their wake remained a path of destruction and little sprouts of dirt that were expelled from the broom with every missed smash against the floor.

Miss Quinn wasn't going to stop. And the class never expected her to.

"Here, mousy mousy, come and get some cheese mousy mousy," she coaxed.

"They don't like cheese," sniggered Amy, perched in her chair enjoying the show. "Their sense of taste is way too sensitive for it."

"Be quiet you waffling fool."

"She thinks it's a game Miss Quinn," shouted Jamie, growing brave. "The mouse is playing with you and she's winning."

Amy grinned as the children baited their teacher to the point of explosion.

"A game? Really, well, watch this you four-legged hairball." Miss Quinn fetched an enormous vacuum cleaner from the storeroom.

She turned it on and jammed it under the bookshelf. "Game, set and mouse! Have you any idea how strong this thing is? It could pull paint from the walls."

"Run mouse, run!" screamed Amy over the deafening vacuum suction.

The mouse did indeed run, with Miss Quinn on its tail.

"Go left, under the bags," instructed Amy.

The mouse went left and under the bags.

"Now go right, around the computer. Go to the radiator."

The mouse went right, around the computer then raced towards the radiator. Amy was so relieved. Any other mouse wouldn't understand and may have been killed by now. But thankfully Mrs Gallen was more agile as a rodent than she was as a lady.

"Now go toward the windows. Climb the curtains. **Quick! Quick!"**

The mouse did as instructed.

Miss Quinn sucked up everything in the hunt-exercise books, textbooks, sixteen pencils, a packet of highlighters, a metre stick and three lunch boxes.

"Shut up child," she barked. "You're distracting me!"

"That's it mouse, keep going! Now go around the teacher's table. And around, and around, go, go, go!"

The little mouse, under Amy's guidance, was leading the teacher on a merry dance. Throughout the quest, Miss Quinn was oblivious to one very important fact. The electrical lead from the vacuum was growing shorter and shorter. As they got dizzy, circling the teacher's desk, the wire coiled itself around all four legs, getting tighter and tighter with every lap. Something was going to give way soon, and by the look of determination on the teacher's face, it wouldn't be her.

BOOOOMMMM!

A thunderous bang reverberated around the entire classroom as the four oak legs collapsed in on themselves and sent the table crashing to the ground. But Miss Quinn had only eyes for the mouse. She continued, briefly;

PUUUFFFFF!

The nozzle detached itself from the vacuum cleaner and sent a thick grey mushroom cloud of dirt billowing up into the air. She stood, hunched over and panting. Aghast, she clung to the vacuumless nozzle.

A peculiar moment of silence fell over the room, the dirt cloud stood motionless, the mouse stopped, and the frantic chase ceased.

Slowly the teacher's heartless eyes swept across the room before lingering on Amy. "You!" Her lips curled with disgust as she advanced upon the child. "You intolerable child! Time's up," she said, grabbing Amy by her tie and pulling her close. The brazen woman had snapped.

"I'm sick, Miss," squeaked Amy, faint and struggling for air.

"You are?" replied the teacher, in a high-pitched tone. "How sick?"

"Like really sick. I think I ate too many doughnuts."

Her eyes narrowed on the red-headed girl before her. "Hmmmmm."

"Miss!" chorused the class. "Miss, look!"

"Shut it. I've more important matters," she snapped.

"But Miss."

She turned her eyes only slightly to see a sugar-laced arc of sick split the dusty air like a revoltingly beautiful rainbow. A sinister smile spread slowly across the woman's face.

"Two for the price of one, come on I'll take you both home!" she smirked.

17
Fear is for the Brave

There are many moments in our lives when we are called into action. Dare we be brave, or shall we cower and run away? Amy faced such a moment right now. A moment that could define the rest of her life, and she was terrified. And yet she was pleased. Being scared, nervous, and trembling, are natural reactions. Some people believe that you are born brave, that it is innate. Others firmly believe that it is determined by how you are raised. Amy was always told by her parents that fear is for the brave because cowards never stare it in the eye.

She climbed to her feet and gulped. Her throat had completely dried up. Maybe she was sick. She wouldn't know, having never experienced it before. Miss Quinn shut closed her laptop and grabbed her handbag.

Jamie too rose to his feet. Amy, wide-eyed, could see the look of absolute terror upon his face, but smiled at how brave he too was being. The dark-haired boy pulled his jumper down over his belly and then, biting his bottom lip, strode out in front of the exiting teacher.

"Miss," he croaked.

"Yes, what is it?"

"Miss," he repeated, this time looking at Amy with raised eyebrows.

Amy could tell he was buying her time. Maybe he hoped she would swoop into action and put her powers to use. But she had a plan. And needed Jamie to trust her. She threw him a comforting wink.

Miss Quinn launched a long straight finger into the chest of the sweaty child and began to push. "You need to get out of my way now, boy. Before I do something, *you'll* regret!" She forced Jamie towards his seat and gave him a shove. He stumbled, missed the chair and fell flat on his bottom. "Come on you two!" she fumed, heading towards the door.

Jamie looked up longingly with worry at Amy. She mouthed, "It's okay."

But as she staggered down the corridor, already filling with regret, she wasn't sure everything was okay. Woozy with fear, she looked to the frizzy-haired boy, Ben, alongside her for some sort of reassurance. But then again, he didn't know what was in store and he was much too ill to converse with anyone.

Sitting in the back of Miss Quinn's car Amy thought it best to copy Ben's ailments if she was to be believable. She didn't have to worry about feeling faint. Just thinking about where she was was enough to make her feel woozy. Then she licked the palms of her hands and smeared her face. Ever so quietly she cranked the window down to listen and rested her sweaty forehead against the pane of glass.

Miss Quinn's routine was as brilliant as it was predictable. Ben's parents weren't entirely enthused with the idea of their boy going away on such short notice and took a little persuasion from Miss Quinn. Listening in tentatively, Amy was struck by just how charming her teacher could be. She knew exactly what to say, when to say it and had the parents eating up every delicious word as if it were true. Uncle Jack on the other hand offered no resistance. It was a brief ten-second phone call. And that's when Amy's plan A was abruptly replaced with plan B. Instead, now she took a deep breath, put on a steely-eyed look of determination and continued with the backup plan. *Get into Miss Quinn's lab and the moment she returned to school use her powers and escape with every animal.*

The teacher's house looked much tidier than before. All the takeaway cartons had been binned, the dishes had been washed and even her suitcase looked to be packed and ready to go. *But where was she going? What was she up to now?*

"But this isn't my house, Miss," moaned Ben, in between a fit of dry retching.

"Obviously," snorted Miss Quinn. "I've some special medicine here for you. Then we will have you off to your own bed. As for you Cupples, I've something very special in store for you." With a glint in her eye, she led the pair of children through the house and towards the lab to the rear. "Sit down!"

Amy sat bolt upright in a plastic seat, her eyes buzzing as they followed Miss Quinn around the room. Ben collapsed into his chair, panting and wiping away drool from his chin. Fighting to stay conscious, the noise and smell of caged animals hadn't even registered with him. Amy's tactics weren't very consistent, and she knew it. She slumped down in her chair and began breathing heavily. She hoped her eyes wouldn't betray her true intentions.

"Now Ben," said Miss Quinn. "This won't hurt in the slightest. And it will have you bouncing around in no time." She lifted an injection from many on her worktop and raised it into the light. Studying the precious contents in the vial like a mother might a newborn baby, she carefully nursed the long needle towards Ben and then jabbed it into his neck.

"What are you doing?" said Amy, aghast.

Miss Quinn strode over to the girl and ran a sharp nail down her face before suddenly ripping the whistle from around her neck. "Do you think I'm stupid, child?"

Amy uncontrollably released a short high-pitched yelp. Her whole body was quivering, and it wasn't because she was ill, or pretending to be.

Miss Quinn forcibly grabbed her by the arm and hurdled her across the room towards the cages. **"Get in!"** she ordered.

Amy looked at the curled lip and snarl on the teacher's face and immediately crawled into the cage. A padlock was snapped onto the cage and the key was tossed onto the worktop, agonisingly in sight, but utterly beyond reach. Amy looked around her. The terrified animals were muted by the presence of Miss Quinn, clearly fearful of what she could do next. To her left, curled in a ball, was a little gazelle, on the right was a dog-sized elephant with his trunk cowering between his legs.

"Now watch," said Miss Quinn with relish.

Before her very eyes, Ben began humming pleasantly. The sweat had dried up. He stopped sniffling and quivering, and he was looking altogether healthier. He even started to smile. However, he suddenly then leapt to his feet like he had been electrocuted. He raced off to the corner of the room, fell to the floor and released a blood-curdling scream.

"Damn!" yelled Miss Quinn. "Not again."

A miniature kangaroo, no taller than Amy's knee, returned from the corner instead of Ben. The cute little hopping creature bounced all over the room in search of an escape. Miss Quinn snapped furiously, "Stay!" and Ben did. She swiftly fell onto him and bundled him into a cage.

"Shame, I thought I had it that time," she said, not sounding entirely disappointed at all. The horrid woman withdrew a bottle of perfume from her handbag and sprayed some on herself and into the air. "You lot stink. Shan't be long, I'll see you soon," she added with a condescending wave to Amy before she left.

18
Open the Cages

Amy gritted her teeth and furrowed her brow as she watched the shadow of her cruel teacher sweep up the corridor and out of view. 'You won't see me soon,' she whispered, already moving into position to kick open the cage door.

But just before trying to break free, there was a knock on the only window spilling light into the lab. Amy pressed her face up against the cage to cop a view of Jamie frantically waving. With a protruding finger through the cage bars, she ushered him towards the silver backdoor.

"It's nailed shut," he panted, "she's fixed it!"

Amy shimmed to the back of her cage and was just about to kick the cage door open when she heard Jamie.

"It's okay," he smiled, popping back up at the window. "I've an idea." He removed his backpack, reached inside and produced the little Mrs Gallen mouse.

He raced back to the recently mended door and released the mouse. Together they watched as the tiny mouse scampered through the slightest of gaps between the door frame and the wall.

"The key!" screeched Jamie, tongue almost licking the window as he spoke. "It's on top of the table. Just there," he pointed.

Amy's heart swelled with pride at her best friend's bravery and ingenuity.

In a single bound, and without any further instruction, the grey mouse scaled the legs of the table and pushed the key to the cold tiled floor.

DING!

The key bounced to a rest. Mrs Gallen leapt to the ground and pushed the key within Amy's reach.

She opened the lock, clambered out and darted to the window.

"Miss Quinn has gone back to school. And she knows I rescued the dog and mouse!"

"You mean Mrs Gallen and Principal Thomson," corrected Jamie.

"Yes, yes," she rushed. "But now, now she'll know you're involved too. She'll be out for you next."

Every nerve in Amy's body was tingling furiously, even her flaming red hair appeared to be redder than usual. Twitching with anger, she threw her shoulder into the silver door and sent it crashing to the ground, again.

Jamie ran in to meet his friend.

"You shouldn't have come," said Amy. "It's too dangerous."

Jamie's head lowered like a scolded puppy.

"But I'm glad you did," she smiled. "Right, throw all those injections into your bag."

"All of them?" asked Jamie, holding aloft a rack with around twenty different coloured vials.

"Yeah! It's the medicine she's been testing on everyone she kidnaps. That's why she's been making people sick. Well, she calls it medicine. But the side effects…"

"It turns you into an animal, doesn't it?" interjected Jamie.

"Exactly! You get those, I'm going to release the animals…I mean people." Amy darted around the lab ripping the covers from each cage, releasing a combination of sounds that shook the whole room.

"You're not letting them all out, are you?" asked Jamie, in a tone even he noticed was too high-pitched. "I mean it's fine if you are," he added casually, in a deep manly voice.

"It'll be okay," stressed Amy reaching for the first cage. A furious black bear filled the cage. His thick fur sprouted through the bars and his snout was grunting ferociously. Amy was immediately drawn to his dark eyes. Like all the other animals the moment his eyes fell upon her she could see his relief.

Jamie backed away from the open door and skulked towards the worktop. He leapt up. While his feet dangled, his eyes darted from cage to cage; the little elephant, the prowling tiger, a kangaroo and in the top row was a gazelle, strutting impatiently from one side of the cage to the other.

Silence suddenly fell upon the room, as the clip-clop of high heels neared, sending a shiver racing down Amy's spine. *She should still be in school. Lunchtime isn't over.* But Amy was about to learn that Miss Quinn thought less of teaching than she could imagine.

She continued to swiftly release the latch on every cage and watch as the victims flew, crawled and galloped out the back door and towards freedom. Amy made for the door too; out into the open grass and onto the main road, with animals on either side and her friend to her rear.

The pace finally eased off when the infuriated screams of the vile teacher were drowned out by the sound of traffic.

"That was easier than I thought," she wheezed. "Did you get all those injections, Jamie? One of them might turn the animals back into humans."

There was no response. Without even turning around, worry was already beginning to swell within her. *Where was Jamie?*

"Amy!" came a blood-curdling panicked holler for help. **"Amy!"**

She turned on her heels, so angry she was seeing spots in front of her eyes. In seconds she had sprinted back to the house but as she neared the scene of the rescue mission her heart sank, and a lump stuck in her throat.

Jamie was being led slowly up the path by Miss Quinn, who clipped him on the ear to silence him. The petite woman had her bony claw of a hand upon his shoulder and stopped just short of entering her house. She scanned the street. Amy puffed out her chest and stepped forward from behind a tree to catch the teacher's gaze. The fixed stare lasted for an age before Miss Quinn produced a sinister grin revealing her gleaming sharp teeth.

Pushing Jamie inside first, Miss Quinn entered her house but left the front door ajar.

19
An Open Door

Amy felt so wretchedly guilty. Phoning Uncle Jack would be useless and telling the police was an even bigger waste of time. A teacher turning people into animals. She'd be laughed out of the place. Besides no children were reported missing; they were all away on a school trip, Mrs Gallen was off sick; apparently for two weeks and who would care about a missing principal; especially one so scary that the teachers were pleased to see him absent.

It was on her, and her alone, to do something now. Amy's short sharp breaths left her feeling woozy, no worse than what Jamie was going through though. She staggered forward towards the open door.

An open door? It was just too convenient. Undoubtedly a trap Amy told herself, and one she wasn't going to fall for. She'd wait for Miss Quinn to leave. She'd have to sooner or later, wouldn't she? The minutes dragged by and the house sat in silence. Soon darkness was falling, and the cold night air was creeping in through the still open front door.

It was now or never. Amy placed her hands on the wall, took a long deep breath, looked to the starry night sky above her and willed the bubbling emotions to fuel her powers of invisibility. But she needed to be cautious, otherwise, Jamie could be in greater danger.

132

She did love her new friend. His sense of humour, his optimism and the fact he always believed in her. Now she had to make sure that friendship would last.

Amy discarded her uniform and reflective sequin dress and she stepped out onto the road in full view of Miss Quinn's house. Whilst she could see her warm breath meet the cold air, she wasn't cold; not a shiver or a goose bump. But then again, she couldn't see them anyway. The North American Tree Frog doesn't get cold. A strange ability, but one that now was proving useful. And it was one that her parents knew about. What else did they know?

Those questions were for another time. She clenched her fists and ever so slowly strode up the garden path and into the house. It rested in darkness; the only light offered by a streetlight breaking in between the gaps in the blinds. She continued through the living room and towards the kitchen. Every door was wedged open, inviting her. Despite wanting to turn down the invitation, she pressed on. The only sound present was that of her knocking knees.

Every careful delicate footstep echoed off the bare walls and hard wooden floor. Stepping into the long corridor that lead to the lab, Amy paused and strained her eyes. Something loomed ahead. As she neared, Jamie came into view, causing a yelp to escape from her throat.

Jamie looked peculiar; he wasn't himself. His eyes were drowsy and his heavy head hung so low that his chin rested on his chest. Jamie's feet were tied to the legs of the chair and his arms were bound behind his back. Amy's heart walloped against her chest so hard she thought it may burst out.

She dared to venture forward, unseen and undetected. *But where was Miss Quinn?*

Above Jamie flickered an old bulb, on then off, on then off again. The eerie scene was amplified further by the fact he was covered in chocolate. It was smeared around his face and stained his white shirt. *Had she forced him to eat? Did Miss Quinn make him sick?*

Amy fought the urge to race in and rescue him. She tiptoed on, just a few more steps and she was in the lab. Only the creaking floorboards beneath her feet broke the silence now. Suddenly, as she crossed the threshold of the lab, a crunching sound erupted from below. She looked down to see she had trod on what looked like cornflakes. It was a trap! Her legs froze, unsure whether to advance or retreat. She raised her head slowly to meet Jamie as he stared in her direction. She saw him shake his head, but it was too late. A cloud of Miss Quinn's perfume choked the intrepid girl just before she felt a hard metal object flash across her vision and hit her on the head.

It was pitch black outside. How long had I been out? she wondered. Amy woke up tied to a chair, in an oversized school uniform, with no socks and shoes, and a throbbing headache.

"And there she is, finally awake," taunted Miss Quinn, staring disdainfully at the two children at her mercy. "A neat little trick that, going invisible, like a Crocodile Ice Fish, that transparent little creature even has invisible blood. But you probably already knew that just like I knew you'd try that."

Amy groaned as she turned her neck towards Jamie. He just shrugged his shoulders.

"Oh no, he didn't tell me," said Miss Quinn, speaking slowly and clearly so as not a word was missed. "I know more about you Amy Cupples than you could imagine."

Just hearing the evil woman use her full name sent a shudder up her spine. She began to squirm and move her bound limbs as much as possible from the gaze of the woman. This was the perfect opportunity to use her magnificent strength and break free. Like that of a Hercules beetle who can lift eight hundred and fifty times its body weight. That's like a human lifting ten elephants. But it didn't work. She didn't even have human strength.

She hadn't an ounce of anger, just a tonne of fear and a lot of pain in her head.

"So, you thought you'd get away with my medicines, and my serums, did you?"

"They don't work anyway," yelled Amy defiantly back at the teacher. "I saw you try. They just turn people into animals. And you didn't seem happy about that." She smirked.

"Oh, is that so." Miss Quinn towered over Jamie as he wheezed and spluttered. He was sweating profusely and looking like he was about to vomit at any moment. Without any warning, the woman jabbed a needle into his thigh and emptied the green contents of a vial into the terrified boy.

Amy's eyes were practically all white as she watched Jamie twist and squirm in his chair. His face contorted and his very fingertips shook with pain. He barked like a seal before shrinking into his clothes and out of sight.

20
Headache

"What have you done to him?"

screamed Amy in a panic.

"Relax, relax," droned Miss Quinn, leaning into the pile of clothes that now rested on Jamie's chair. "He's fine. Actually, I don't think he's ever looked better. Don't you agree?" She produced a cute little opossum.

Amy couldn't believe her eyes the first time she saw Ben turned into a kangaroo. But this time it was more personal. A fury was mounting, her cheeks glowed crimson, not a freckle to be seen. But as the blood rushed from her head to her face, she felt dizzy and struggled to focus.

"Just a little dose. It doesn't last. I've got much more special treatment in store for you two children."

137

As suddenly as he vanished, Jamie grew out of the opossum and back into his chair. He wore a confused and startled look on his face, particularly when he looked down and realised that he wasn't fully dressed. Red-faced he shuffled back into his uniform as Miss Quinn approached to tie him up again.

"I think you'll find it does work. Are you still sick?" Miss Quinn asked Jamie.

"No, I feel great now."

"You see. It just has…" she paused, "a few tiny side effects."

"Tiny?" said Amy incredulously. "You just turned him into an opossum."

"A what?" screeched Jamie. "An opossum? Isn't that like a rat?"

"No!" snapped Miss Quinn, lowering herself to look him in the eye. "It's a marsupial."

"And it's almost invulnerable to snake poisons," Amy added.

"You certainly are your parent's child."

"Yeah, and they'll come looking for me. Just like the parents of the other missing children." Amy lifted her groggy head to look the teacher in the eye. "And all roads lead back to you. You're done for."

"You still don't get it, do you? Just like your little friend can't remember being an opossum, the rest won't remember what they were turned into, never mind where they were. They'll turn up in a few days, or hours, with a lot fewer clothes, but human again. Another unwanted, but helpful, side effect."

"See, the serum doesn't work then does it?" argued Amy.

"This serum is made up of a concoction of animal DNA. Only the strongest and most resistant to disease. I just haven't managed to get the balance right, not yet. But your parents did, didn't they?" she whispered, moving her hungry eyes towards the red-haired child.

Amy could feel a cold sweat drip down her forehead. She shook her throbbing head and forced her eyes to focus.

"Oh my, oh my, you don't know do you?" the woman purred. "Ever been sick Amy? I bet not."

Amy croaked, "And?"

"And? And that's because a serum courses through your blood. And at the minute it is busy trying to heal your sore head. It'll be a while before you have any of those abilities again," she smirked. "With no strength, no powers, you'll be doing exactly as I say," Miss Quinn preached, she began tracing her fingernails along the bars of the empty cages. "I've waited a long time for this. Your parents have cost me millions. Do you know how much a serum like that could make? Instead, I'm teaching, teaching!" The enraged woman wheeled around and began circling the two trapped children. "Do you realise how beneath me teaching is? Vile, snotty, disobedient children. And idiot principals whom I'm expected to perform for. Schools have been good for one thing and one thing only.."

"Subjects to test your serum on," interjected Amy.

"Precisely, bright child! And now with you here I can complete my serum." She picked up a needle and ran its sharp end along the length of Amy's arm. "Inside you, my dear, is the answer. The final piece to my puzzle. I've got the data, the research.."

"On the laptop," interrupted Amy.

"Yeah, what's the deal with taking her parent's laptop? Was your one useless?" piped up Jamie. "Mine is ancient too. So slow and…"

"Quiet!" Miss Quinn spat. "You buffoon."

Jamie instantly pursed up his lips and turned a shade paler.

"It's my laptop really," drawled the woman. "You see I was a work colleague of your parents."

Amy remembered back to the laptop being used in class and the screen projected behind Miss Quinn. Cupples and associate- Disease Cure Research. Miss Quinn must have been the associate.

"We had worked together, for years, on an antidote," continued the torturous teacher. "We were close. Could have cured millions of diseases. Then suddenly, one day I show up for work and they're gone. Not so much as a note, a letter, a phone call, nothing. Gone with the laptop, the research and years of work. But now, I have it back. My serum has been getting closer and closer to being perfect. All I need is blood samples of the serum working. Then I can replicate it. And would you look here, I have an ample supply," she grinned raising the needle above her head about to stab it into Amy's arm.

"There's no point," interrupted Jamie again, nonchalantly. "Skin like an armadillo."

A vein on the side of the villainous woman's head began to visibly pound. She looked to the ceiling pondering her next move. "That's something your sneaky parents would do all right."

"Genius," Amy whispered to her friend. "And do you know what, I'm suddenly feeling much better. That headache has gone already."

"Do you know their shell can deflect some bullets," he smiled.

Miss Quinn took a step back from Amy and fixed her gaze on the trembling boy before her. There was a tension in the air, as thick and as indistinct as the perfume smell. Then without warning the teacher broke into a fit of hysterical laughter. "Well then, if I can't draw blood, I'll be doing all my testing on you Mr Hannaway," she cackled. "We are going to spend some quality time together, testing serum, after serum, after serum, on the one little guinea pig I have left."

Miss Quinn suddenly whipped her head around to Amy. "And you, you can watch it all." She kept her unblinking eyes upon the girl as she menacingly began to pat Jamie's tear-stained cheek with the back of her hand.

21
Taking the Bait

Amy gulped. It was hard and dry. "My parents were clearly the brains of the operation. They made the antidote, the serum you can't. That explains why you worked for them; you were only a colleague. And now they've even moved on to doing more worthwhile work, like saving endangered animals. Do you know over the last forty years fifty per cent of all species have been declared extinct?"

Miss Quinn moved closer still, her eyes narrow and her mouth twitching. **"Blah, blah,** blah."

Amy closed her eyes, and then slowly opened them, choosing bravery over fear. Miss Quinn was so close she was positive that she saw the little spark of lightning that illuminated her eyes and brought her to life. A plan popped into her head, an almighty plan, one that would teach her a lesson, her final lesson. It was genius really, but it had to be played just right otherwise she would suspect a trap.

"Their old work is finished," continued Amy, "filed away in the garage with all the other notes and blood samples."

Miss Quinn paused and looked at her. Her cold eyes sank into the girl. "Blood samples?" she replied, raising one incredulous eyebrow. "What blood samples?"

"I've said too much."

"And you're going to say more," she snapped. "Otherwise your precious friend here won't be seen again! Well, not as a human anyway"

"Okay, okay," rushed Amy. "It's in the garage, of our house. It's full of old laboratory equipment and a huge fridge freezer."

"Really?" Miss Quinn smiled.

"To be honest I thought a smart woman like you would have taken everything you needed when you were there stealing the laptop." Amy was baiting the woman. And she could tell by the smile creeping across Miss Quinn's face that it was working.

"You had better not be lying to me child," Miss Quinn spat.

"No, no, I promise," she lied. "The fridge was full of test tubes, syringes, microscopes and blood in between sheets of glass."

"Jackpot! That's exactly the stuff! I knew your parents weren't foolish enough to destroy it all." She was giddy with excitement, already on her feet and putting on a long black hooded coat.

Jamie's jaw had dropped so much it was virtually resting on his chest. Amy threw him a nod and a smile. He knew instantaneously that she had a plan.

"So, you'll let us go then?" pleaded Amy. "I mean you have everything you need."

"You're a smart one. There may be hope for you yet. So of course, I will. Why wouldn't I?" she smirked.

Jamie gave a loud snort and was swiftly silenced by an unpleasant smile Miss Quinn flashed in his direction.

Miss Quinn sauntered up behind Amy and placed her hands on the masking tape around her wrists. Amy readied herself. The moment the restraints were in any way loose she was going to make a run for it.

"You must think I'm an idiot." She pulled a roll of tape from her coat pocket and added another layer to her wrists, cutting off the blood supply and turning her fingers purple. She shuffled Amy's chair towards Jamie's and tied them together, back to back. "You have been ever so helpful. But I'll be off now." Her twisted smile widened as she left.

Miss Quinn had taken the bait. Amy never genuinely expected to be released, but it was worth a shot. At least, it had succeeded in buying her and Jamie some time to try and break free.

"You haven't really given her everything she wants?" asked Jamie, panting as he wrestled with the tape around his wrists. "Is there actually a fridge freezer in the garage?"

"Yeah."

"Yeah?" interrupted Jamie, incredulously.

"It's massive. A chest freezer, like the type chips are kept inside in a supermarket. It used to be in my parent's office. But now it's in the garage…"

"Not with the blood samples in it?"

"No," laughed Amy, "just ice cream."

"Ice cream you say, well what are we waiting for? Let's get out of these chairs. Can you use your strength?" suggested Jamie. "My arms are killing me."

But she couldn't. A pulsing headache was causing a tingle behind her eyes. "I can't," she replied. "It's still not working."

Jamie looked to the ground forlornly.

"We'll have to work together to get out of this one," Amy added. She twisted her neck to try and look at her friend. "Ready? Side to side, copy me."

Together they began rocking the two attached chairs, slowly building up momentum. Right, then left, right a little further and then left a little further still, before eventually tipping over the plastic chairs. The seats burst upon impact leaving them both free to squirm and wriggle until the bonds around their feet were kicked over and off the chair legs.

"Turn around," they both said in unison. The two friends smiled at each other as their plans synced up.

Back to back, they started to unwrap the rolls of tape that bound them.

"I've an idea. Open your bag." Amy raced to the worktop that lined the right of the lab and grabbed her parent's laptop. "We'll need proof if we are to be believed after all of this. Stick that in your school bag with the serums."

"So, what next?" asked Jamie.

"Next? I've a cool plan. We are going to put that evil woman and her plans on ice!"

22
Dogs as Horses

Jamie led as they tore away from Miss Quinn's house. Amy, panting and woozy, was still nursing a throbbing headache and struggled to breathe. It didn't help that the oversized uniform she woke up in was soaked in the undeniable stench of the villainous teacher's perfume and was slowly suffocating her.

"Did you like my armadillo fact?" panted Jamie.

"It was brilliant, but how did.."

"I looked it up. I knew it would impress you."

Amy stopped in her tracks and smiled before her attention returned to her throbbing head. "No speed and a sore head. It's no good. My house is miles away. We'll never get there in time." Amy paced around, twisting one end of her hair around her finger. "Hold on, hold on, I know!" she finally announced. "Do you know the way to Principal Thomson's house from here?"

"Do you think he's human again? Could he help?" Jamie asked, hopeful.

"Maybe, I don't know, but I've got an idea if he's not."

*

It didn't take long to reach the principal's house and the moment they swung open a squeaking gate the magnificent huge dog, Seamus, came bounding down the path towards them. Jamie, much to Amy's surprise, was first to greet him.

The duo raced to the back of the house to find a very sad muscular dog curled up in a ball at the foot of the doorstep.

Amy tentatively stepped forward and approached the dog, "Principal Thomson."

But he didn't stir. His ears didn't even flicker.

"I know this must be hard," began Amy, sensitive and serious. "But the serum Miss Quinn injected you with, it won't last. You'll be yourself again soon."

Principal Thomson's square head shot up like a dog's does when he's heard the word 'walkies.' He stood up tall, stretched and then strode towards the brave girl.

"And, you won't remember ever being a dog or what Miss Quinn did to you. That's why we need your help now. To get some revenge and stop her."

Principal Thomson's dark brown eyes and twitching ears made it obvious he understood every word. He was still himself, in there, in the body of that frightening dog. He stood before Amy, tail wagging, and ready to help.

"We need to get across the town. To my house, and quick."

"Well he can hardly drive us, Amy," interrupted Jamie, resting an elbow on Seamus' back. "More chance of riding him like a horse."

"Exactly!"

"Ha, good one. Almost had me believing you."

Principal Thomson had already turned around and presented himself to be climbed upon. Amy without hesitation leapt on the dog's back and clung to the fur on his neck for safety.

"Nope, no chance," insisted Jamie. "Not happening, not today."

But as the reluctant boy walked away, Seamus had other ideas. The intelligent Irish wolfhound, with his head stooped, tackled Jamie from behind. In one flowing movement he launched his head between the boy's legs, threw his head back and tumbled him onto his back.

Jamie screamed in a high-pitched tone that could have shattered glass. When he finally stopped, he looked across at Amy with a forced smile.

"Ready then?" she asked.

He dug his nails into the dog's thick fur and nodded.

Together they galloped down the street, racing out onto the main road. The cars leapt aside and stalled to stare at the extraordinary sight. Amy clung on to Principal Thomson, the wind blowing through her long red hair and smiled through gritted teeth. Jamie, atop Seamus, was less graceful. He swung from side to side, like a fence swaying in a storm that could keel over at any moment.

The dogs turned right and followed a narrow, twisting road up a long steep hill. At the top, they stopped and paused outside a lonely house illuminated by a solitary light in the adjoining garage. One-half of the garage's double doors were open, and the fluorescent light spilt out onto the driveway.

Amy's eyes were stinging but the needling pain in her head had ceased. Reaching for the bump on her head, it had shrunken in size. *Would her powers be back?*

Facing Miss Quinn without them was a different prospect. But with Jamie by her side, it was one she could face.

Jamie clung to the back of Amy's jumper as the duo slithered towards the garage. Amy took a deep breath and dared to look in. She watched in jittery silence, as Miss Quinn, fearlessly, with no concern about getting caught, was spinning around the garage like a tornado, causing havoc.

Creeping over boxes, packaging and black bags; Amy cautiously moved in for a better view. The garage was quite large. It stretched much further back than the eye would think.

"What are you doing?" whispered Jamie.

"Look! This is my chance."

Miss Quinn had lifted the enormous glass lid and rested it against the wall. She was bent over peering into the fridge freezer.

Amy suddenly took off. Mowing down the teacher, with her arms outstretched, she was about to push the dreadful woman headfirst into the appliance.

But with frightful suddenness, Jamie trod on some bubble wrap. The sound was deafening, like gunshots in a war. Miss Quinn stopped immediately. She whipped her head around just in time to see Amy advance. The woman stepped to one side, threw her hand on the back of the girl's head and sent her tumbling into the fridge freezer.

"Where there's one, there's another," she purred. **"Get out here now, child."**

Jamie revealed himself from behind some cardboard boxes.

"In!" ordered Miss Quinn, pointing to the fridge freezer. "No blood samples. Nothing. You'll regret that little stunt!" She showed a smile, wide enough to reveal black fillings that Amy hadn't seen before.

23
Trapped Cold

Amy and Jamie crouched next to each other in the fridge freezer panting and trembling. Miss Quinn slammed the clear glass lid closed and slid across a latch to ensure it stayed that way. It was quickly obvious that the appliance was still switched on. The hum of the fan sprouting out cold air rang in their ears and every breath they took clouded the confined space.

"How's your...your..h.h.h.head?" chattered Jamie. "Pppowers back yet?"

Amy knew the answer without trying to break free. The goosebumps racing along her arms confirmed she still had no abilities. *Would they ever come back?*

"N..n...no," she replied, rubbing the bump on her head. "Soon I think," she added, noticing the bump had almost vanished.

Jamie tried to smile but his frozen face showed little movement. He tried to prize open a tub of ice cream but failed. "The sooner your s.s.s.strength is back, the..the..the...better."

Amy hugged her arms tightly around her chest, barely able to stop herself from shivering. Miss Quinn was clattering away, banging and kicking things, tossing boxes and emptying drawers. Amy wiped the glass clear and craned her neck to stare quizzically at her. *What was she doing?*

"There's got to be something here!" muttered Miss Quinn, with real venom in her tone. Her face had gone purple and the veins on her neck were standing out so far that they threatened to pop like a stood upon grape.

Miss Quinn returned to the fridge freezer and peered into the two trapped frozen children. She menacingly tapped the glass to get their attention.

"Back to my lab it is. We're going to have some fun together."

The horrid woman's words spun around Amy's head like a cobweb, her beady little eyes staring through the glass like a spider about to bite.

"Let us..o..o..out!" hissed Jamie, with glassy eyes. "You w..w…won't get away with this. You w..w…w… won't!"

"Ha! My dear child I already have," snorted Miss Quinn, "There will be no evidence. Anyone injected with my serum will have no memory of the event. Fortunate that," she shrieked. "And you two won't be around to tell anyone." She cackled as she began to wheel the fridge freezer towards the open door.

The fridge freezer abruptly halted with a devastating jolt. It was still plugged into the wall!

With an almighty tug, Miss Quinn ripped the socket from the wall, sending electric sparks dancing in the air. Then she casually wheeled the glassy tomb outside into the vacant driveway.

Fear built up inside Amy's chest, threatening to explode from her mouth in a terrified scream. But then she heard familiar voices. With cold air still whipping around her legs and bare feet, she tried to push open the lid. Jamie placed his blue hands alongside hers and pushed. Their efforts succeeded only in raising the lid a few inches. Enough to take a sharp intake of night air and see who owned those voices.

Amy's eyes welled up.

"Joanne?" said Dad, incredulously.

'Joanne?' mouthed Amy. *So, they were colleagues, they do know each other. If that was true, then maybe it's true about the serum. Maybe that's the source of these powers,* thought the trapped girl.

"Miss Quinn to you, if you please," she retorted.

"Quinn?" chimed in Mum. "As in Amy's teacher Miss Quinn?"

"Who is it?" asked Jamie through chattering teeth. He suddenly got a burst of hope and began thrashing the lid violently.

Miss Quinn smashed the glass top, startling the frozen pair.

"Well, well, well," sneered Miss Quinn. "How was Borneo, Patrick? Back so soon?"

"I assume we have you to thank for that wasted trip," replied Dad.

"What are you doing here, Joanne?" asked Mum. "And what are you doing with our fridge?"

The two friends mustered every ounce of fight remaining and pushed the lid open a few more inches. **"Dad!"** Amy cried. **"Mum!"**

"Amy's mum, Amy's Dad," yelled Jamie.

"Amy?" screamed Mum. She took off like a catapulted rock towards her daughter.

"Ah, ah, ah, just stay back," Miss Quinn purred coolly. "Or else."

The fridge freezer started to move forward again. It rested to a stop on the footpath outside of the house. Amy knew exactly where they were and knew they couldn't move. The sharp incline told her they were tottering at the top of the steep hill.

"It will be okay, sweetheart, it'll be all okay," Dad reassured her.

As the fridge precariously tilted back and forth Amy scampered to the top of the unit, weighing it down and keeping them balanced, for the moment.

Miss Quinn had devilishly positioned herself where she'd have all the power.

Hearing the conversation between the trio outside it was clear that Amy's life was a bargaining tool.

"Come on Joanne," yelled Dad from outside, "don't do anything silly. Just tell us what you want."

"Do you know how long it has taken me," she retorted. "How many schools I went through? How many snotty kids I have had to teach? But finally, I found you. I knew I would find the right Amy Cupples eventually. And what a child she was.."

"Was?" gulped Mum.

"Oh, I'm sorry Margaret. I meant *is* of course."

A fearful panic gripped hold of Amy. She looked to her right to see it was Jamie; he had thrown his arms around her and was squeezing.

"Ah little Amy," snarled Miss Quinn. "What a peculiar child you have." The dainty woman's dark eyes fell upon the fridge freezer she was leaning against and she began salivating.

"She's special. One in a million," defended Dad, stepping closer to his wife and placing an arm around her. "A miracle!"

"Oh, I do not doubt that she is a miracle. Living proof our serum works," interrupted Miss Quinn.

Amy sat curled up, ear pricked, with bated breath only an earshot away, frantically twisting her hair around her little finger. *I knew it,* she thought.

"Joanne, look, we don't want any trouble," sobbed Mum.

"Bit late for that, isn't it, Margaret? By my reckoning, you have already got yourself into quite a bit of trouble. Testing a serum on your daughter, tut tut. But I'll tell you what, you give me what I want, and I'll be on my way."

"And what is it you want?" asked Dad sternly, it was clear anger and impatience were growing within him.

"Just what I'm owed. The research, the samples, everything I need to replicate the serum."

"You're obsessed; you need to move on."

"You mean like you did," drawled Miss Quinn.

"But the side effects, Joanne," interjected Mum.

"I know, brilliant, aren't they?" beamed the teacher. "I can charge even more."

"And if we don't?" asked Dad.

"Well, your precious daughter and her friend will be going on a little trip." She smirked as she nodded down the sharp steep hill.

"Okay, okay," stressed Mum, rushing into the open garage and returning with a briefcase. "I can't find the laptop, but here are vials of successful serum."

"Oh, don't worry about the research on the laptop, I've got that…"

"No, you don't!" yelled Jamie from inside the fridge freezer. "I do!"

Miss Quinn flung open the lid and reached inside. She pulled Jamie up by his tie and threw her face into his. "Where is it?" she spat.

Jamie just pointed to the bag still on his back. The villainous woman never took her eyes off the boy as she reached around and withdrew the laptop from his school bag.

Amy's eyes bounced between her parents. All three pairs were tearful, but a furrowed brow hid a wave of anger behind them.

"Now you've got what you want," said Dad. "Just let them go."

"Just let them go, not a bad idea that."

Amy suddenly felt the fridge lid close on them and sway into motion. The appliance rocketed down the steep hill like a torpedo. Together the friends were flung to the roof of the unit at a frightening pace. Amy heard her back smash and crack and the pain shot through her body and down her legs like an electric shock.

160

Jamie's stomach flipped. They had to fight just to hold back a retch tickling at their throat. This was it! They were going to collide with the concrete wall and be pulverised into a million pieces.

24
Dad Too?

The enormous white bullet shot down the hill. Amy and Jamie were rattling around inside like two unfortunate peas in a maraca. The lid flew open with such velocity that the hinges snapped with a moan, sending it gliding through the air like a frisbee.

Amy dared to stand up. She had to do something, anything, and she had to do it now. Her eyes stung and her long red hair flapped violently as the gushing wind pelted her face. She glanced towards her friend who was spread like a starfish, pushing against the walls of the fridge freezer, as white as the appliance itself. A terror was beginning to nestle in the pit of her stomach. The throbbing head had stopped and as she squeezed the sides of the fridge, she felt the walls crush a little under the pressure. *My strength's back!*

The parked cars, trees and houses all whooshed past in a blur. But as she turned to look back up the hill another blurry object was fast approaching. *Dad?*

Dad hurdled down the hill and towards the fridge. With a wry smile, he overtook the speeding box and grabbed a hold of the front. He dug his feet into the ground and the fridge freezer began to slow down.

Jamie, feeling the change in pace, peeked his head up. "Wait, your Dad has superpowers too?"

The fridge gently came to a stop, just yards from a brick wall. Jamie, shaking and sweaty, clambered out and gawped at Amy's father as she fell straight into his open arms.

"How did you?" she began.

Dad just smiled, "All in good time, my love. But look- Come on!"

At the top of the hill, Mum was wrestling with Miss Quinn, determined to stop the evil woman from escaping.

Dad crouched down, tucking his bottom towards his heels and placed his fingertips on the ground. He took a final look at his daughter and winked before exploding into the air and landing halfway up the hill.

Amy watched in awe. "Klipspringer," she yelled. "They can jump ten times their body height."

"No, a flea in fact," Dad called back down with a grin. "They can jump.."

"150 times their height," interrupted Amy. *Strength and jumping too? Was Miss Quinn lying?*

"Come on Amy," shouted Dad. "Just use your emotions."

Did I inherit my abilities? What about the serum? Her mind was dizzy with questions.

But they could wait. Amy looked ahead at Miss Quinn fighting with Mum. An instant anger ignited inside her. She imitated Dad's launch position.

BOOM! She exploded up the hill, leaving behind a cloud of dust and stones in the air.

"Ah ha, I'll take that," said Miss Quinn, triumphantly. She brushed Mum aside, sending her towards the ground and headed back down the hill towards her parked car. As she walked down, Amy and Dad sprang over her head. Goggling the sight above her, Miss Quinn didn't see Jamie's brave actions.

The sweaty boy, still clambering up the hill, defiantly reached into his schoolbag and withdrew a vial of serum. He ran full pelt toward the callous teacher and jabbed the needle into her.

Amy's heart swelled with pride. For Jamie's fear was no longer a headwind holding him back, it now was a tailwind that spurred him on. All eyes fell upon Miss Quinn as she flapped around on all fours. The woman's neck suddenly snapped up like the bough of a branch snow had just fallen from. Her deathly stare was fixed upon the approaching Amy. The teacher began to growl all the while sneakily inching towards her prey. With each step, she transformed into a terrifyingly wild tiger. Amy froze; her mouth dry and her feet locked to the ground. Dad bolted towards her as Miss Quinn padded forward, claws exposed and ready to strike.

Amy saw Jamie frantically rummaging around in his backpack. With the streetlights offering the only light, Jamie couldn't see just how close Miss Quinn was. Any moment now she'd be within striking distance.

"That's it, Jamie, throw another serum," screeched Amy, "Inject her again."

Miss Quinn swung around with such velocity that her tail whipped across the ankles of Dad and Amy like a skipping rope and knocked them over. Miss Quinn as a tiger would have been beautiful if she wasn't so frightening. Her vibrant colours and stunning size made her a marvellous sight to behold.

Jamie withdrew two more vials of serum. He dared not get any closer. So, the first, a blue vial, he held in his right hand like a dart and with precision sent it sailing through the air towards the advancing tiger. Miss Quinn jinked to the left and nonchalantly avoided the missile. Jamie took the remaining vial in his quivering hand and threw it as hard as he could. The injection spun violently through the air, but unfortunately the wrong end hit the tiger square on the nose. Miss Quinn flashed her razor-sharp teeth and pressed on towards an ample feed.

Amy mustered all the courage she possessed to save her only friend. She broke free from her dad's grasp and picked up the misplaced blue vial. Without hesitation, she leapt onto the tiger's back. Miss Quinn bucked and jumped. She flipped and twisted. The tiger pushed Amy against the wall and shook with all her might to dislodge the girl. But Amy was not for shifting, she forced the sharp needle through the teacher's fur and pressed on the plunger.

Miss Quinn collapsed to the floor writing in pain. She curled up into a ball and then began to shrink, smaller and smaller, and smaller still; until nothing remained but a cute little mouse. Dad bent down to pick up the mouse but received a nasty bite before the furry creature scuttled off towards a crack in the wall.

25
Use the Serum

"I am so happy you're safe, Sweet Pea," said Mum in between kissing every part of her daughter's face. "Don't you ever do that again! What on earth were you thinking? Don't you know you're lucky to be alive?!"

As Amy winced and tried to pull free, she considered how worry does strange things to a person. One moment Mum was yelling at her and the next she was crying tears of joy.

"I'm fine. I had to, Mum."

"Ahem, I?" interrupted Jamie, as he neared the trio.

"I mean, *we* had to. We need to stop her. There's no way I wanted to move schools again."

"Don't you worry about moving schools, Chicken."

"Good, coz I ain't going through all this again just to make a friend," added Jamie with a smirk.

"There will be no need for that," began Dad. "Especially now that you can control your powers. And besides, you've seen to Miss Quinn. I can't imagine she'll be back anytime soon."

"You did it too, Dad," said Amy.

"A superhero family," chirruped Jamie. "I just knew it"

"Yeah good point," said Amy. "I'd almost forgotten you have these abilities too, Dad. Have you, Mum? Are they genetic? Was she lying about that serum?" She stared into her Mum's loving blue eyes, knowing they would reveal the truth.

"Just me and you I'm afraid," Dad stated. "Nothing genetic about them. You see our work was ground-breaking. We worked with lots of wild and wonderful animals and kept them all in our lab at home. We created a mixture of animal DNA, and we were on the verge of curing all known diseases and poisons known to man. Could you imagine, Amy, a world free of disease? No illness, no poison that can't be cured. But Joanne had other ideas. She wasn't interested in the greater good the serum would do; she was obsessed with getting rich. We couldn't allow it to happen. We had countless arguments about the issue. We were actually arguing when you were attacked."

The young girl's eyes grew large with intrigue, "Attacked?"

"Attacked? By who? I'll stop them for you," interjected Jamie, eyes as wide as his open mouth. "I could have stopped them. Bet I could"

Mum smiled, "You're a great friend Jamie."

"The best friend," added Amy.

Jamie blushed and looked to his feet before piping up, "So who attacked Amy?"

"You see those scars on your neck…" began Dad.

"I was bitten by poisonous snakes or spiders, and you had to cure me with the serum," said Amy, smiling.

"Exactly, but how did you…"

"Just something Miss Quinn said," replied Amy.

"So clever, nothing gets by you," gushed Mum. "Even as a toddler, you were inquisitive. You managed to open the animal cages in our lab one day."

"Amy opened cages? Never!" grinned Jamie. "That's a great origin story you know."

"A what?" asked Mum.

"Oh, he loves his comics. So, how come I don't remember this?" asked Amy

"I'm not surprised, my Love. You were unconscious and running a fever, covered in poisonous bites. One boa was constricting itself around your body, while another was widening its jaw to launch an attack."

Amy moved closer to her parents. Her eyes were wide and her mouth was open. But not as wide as Jamie, he was salivating at the idea. It sounded like the script of a movie, a superhero movie. 'A toddler survives a deadly attack; thanks to a serum her parents had created. Only the untested serum has quite unusual side effects.'

"And that's when you used that serum you made with Miss Quinn, to save me."

"It is, my little teacake," said Mum. "But your Dad wouldn't let me use it on you. Not before he tested it on himself. To check it was safe."

Dad smiled bashfully.

Amy threw her arms around her Dad. Mum joined in and soon both parents were sobbing. Amy felt like the filling in a soggy sandwich.

"That's a brilliant story and all," stated Jamie, picking up the briefcase and laptop that Miss Quinn had discarded. "But everyone knows that a superhero needs a sidekick. And I know just the person."

26
Not a Pet

In the days that followed Amy and Jamie were inseparable. Despite his constant requests, Amy's parents understandably never injected the boy with any serum. He remained a normal child without any superpowers. To Amy though, his loyalty, humour and kindness were more powerful than any superpower you could desire. And it didn't bother Jamie that Amy's abilities had all but disappeared. She did not need them anymore. And why would she? She had a permanent school, a loving family and a best friend.

Within days every pupil was back in school. And, as Miss Quinn predicted, nobody had any knowledge or memory of where they had been or what had happened. Mrs Gallen resumed her rightful place as the class teacher. And even though she had developed a strange dislike towards brooms and hoovers, she was as pleasant as ever. Even more so when she was nibbling on some cheese.

PE lessons were no longer dreaded. Principal Thomson left it to the teacher, which made for much more fun lessons. Instead, the enormous man took to walking his dog, Seamus, around the school grounds. He was seen lavishing his dog with attention and treats, and he didn't care who saw him. On the rare occasion, he did yell at someone, it was because he spied a dog owner not picking up dog poo as they walked by the school.

Conor Phillips had even changed. Something must have stuck from the whole experience. He was no longer a bully. You could go as far as to say he was friendly; even picking Amy and Jamie to be on his team, on occasion. The two friends couldn't help but laugh when they were told to 'stop horsing around with Conor and get back to work.'

*

One Saturday night at the end of the month Amy's parents summoned her to the kitchen. She knew this day would come. She walked in apprehensively and sat at the table. There was a moment of silence. They all stared at each other, then smiled.

Dad stretched out his hand, "Okay, Pet."

"She's not a pet." Mum elbowed her husband in the ribs. "You're not a pet, my Chicken," she reassured Amy.

"Relax, Mum," she responded rolling her eyes. "So, am I going to see this full list? I'm dying to see what creatures' DNA is in my blood."

"Now before we do this, you have to remember that it doesn't change a thing. It's not what you can do or can't do that determines who you are, it's what's in your heart. And you my love, you are the best of us all. With your heart, you could always do anything you

172

wanted. You, Amy, are the most unique individual in the world and your mum and I could not be any prouder of you, young lady." Mum became a little teary as Dad went on. "Now this list is quite lengthy. There are a great many animals in it, some you may never have heard of.."

"Hey," interrupted Amy, "I know every animal."

Dad smiled and continued, "Well keep in mind some of them will never affect you."

"Some? Your Dad means most," interjected Mum. "But whatever we face, now and in the future, we face together, as a family."

Dad slid the laptop across the table in front of Amy. She took a long deep breath, looked into her parents' hopeful eyes then began to read the list aloud.

The End

Printed in Great Britain
by Amazon